ESCAPING DARKNESS

ESCAPING DARKNESS 10

TYNDALE KiDS

TYNDALE HOUSE PUBLISHERS, INC., CAROL STREAM, ILLINOIS

RED ROCK MYSTERIES

Visit Tyndale's website for kids at www.tyndale.com/kids.

TYNDALE is a registered trademark of Tyndale House Publishers, Inc.

Tyndale Kids logo is a trademark of Tyndale House Publishers, Inc.

Escaping Darkness

Designed by Jacqueline L. Nuñez

Edited by Lorie Popp

Published in association with the literary agency of Alive Communications, Inc., 7680 Goddard Street, Suite 200, Colorado Springs, CO 80920.

Scripture quotations are taken from the *Holy Bible,* New Living Translation, copyright © 1996, 2004 by Tyndale House Foundation. Used by permission of Tyndale House Publishers, Inc., Carol Stream, Illinois 60188. All rights reserved.

For manufacturing information regarding this product, please call 1-800-323-9400.

Library of Congress Cataloging-in-Publication Data

Jenkins, Jerry B.
   Escaping darkness / Jerry B. Jenkins, Chris Fabry.
     p. cm. — (Red Rock mysteries ; 10)
Summary: Twins Ashley and Bryce get involved in another mystery when they observe strange goings-on near the alpaca farm, and, meantime, their school is imbroiled in a controversy over an annual day of public prayer.
   ISBN 978-1-4143-0149-5 (sc)
   [1. Christian life—Fiction. 2. Schools—Fiction. 3. Drug dealers—Fiction. 4. Illegal aliens—Fiction.
5. Twins—Fiction. 6. Colorado—Fiction. 7. Mystery and detective stories.] I. Fabry, Chris, date. II. Title.
   PZ7.J4138Esc 2006
   [Fic]—dc22   2005025246

Printed in the United States of America

17   16   15   14
 9   8   7   6   5   4

This book is dedicated to kids who cry for help.

Thanks to Amy Disselkoen for linguistic help.

" DO or DO NOT.
There is no try. "

Yoda

"As long as ALGEBRA is taught
in school, there will be PRAYER in school."

Cokie Roberts

"Calling ATHEISM a religion
is like calling BALD a hair color."

Don Hirschberg

"I once wanted to become an
atheist, but I GAVE UP—
they have no holidays."

Henny Youngman

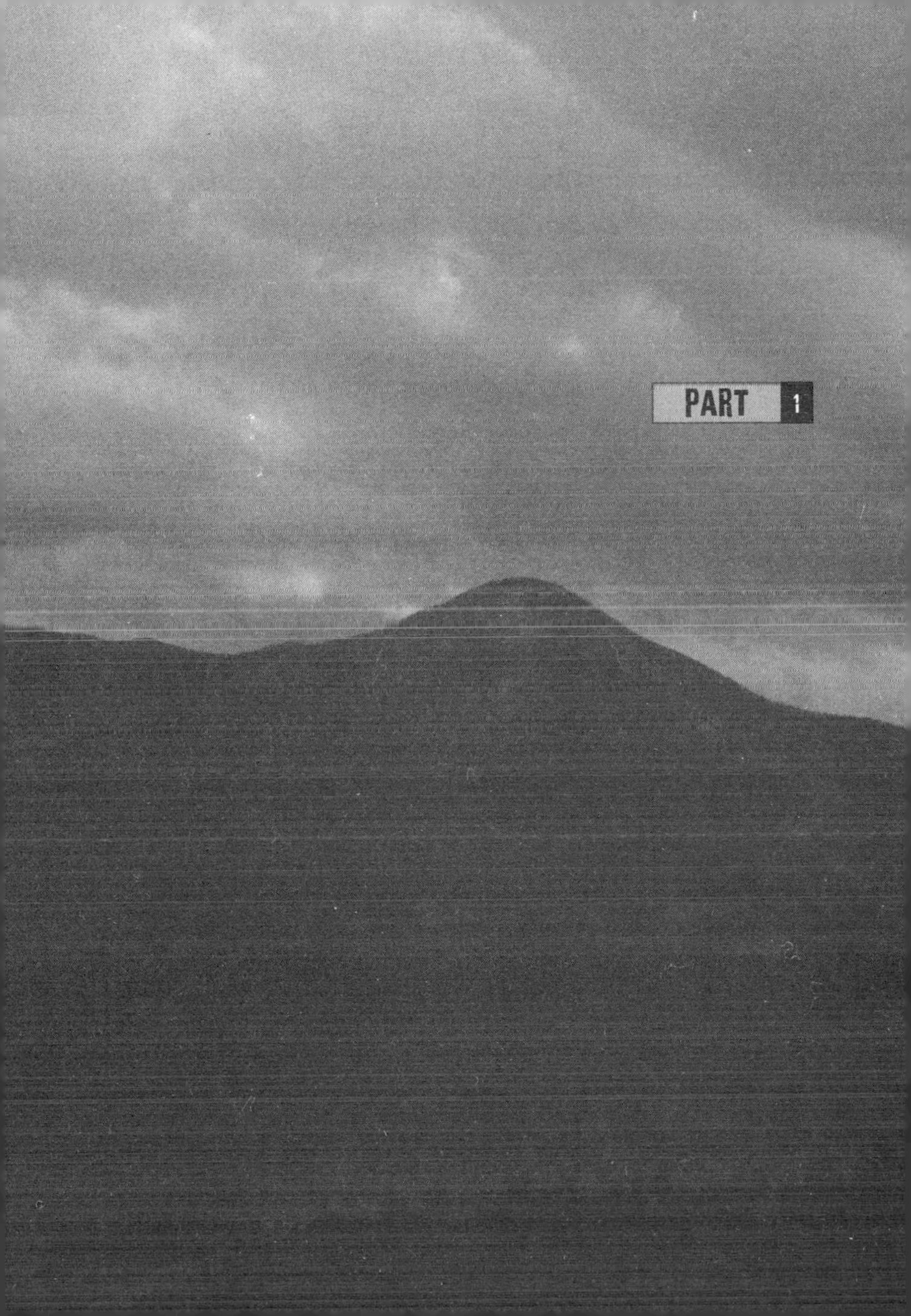

PART 1

BEFORE

Darkness was her constant friend. An inky, black nothing. She had stopped counting the days, stopped trying to remember when she hadn't felt hungry. Trapped. Alone.

During the day a sliver of light pierced the door, and she strained to see more of it. Beautiful daylight.

Before she had been locked away, before her cries for help, she remembered daylight, soft and pure and warm. Now it felt a world away.

What parents could do this to their own flesh and blood? Were they really her parents? How could people be so mean? so uncaring?

The one bright spot was her brother. He brought her food late at night or when their parents weren't around. Broken pieces of sandwich. Crackers. Once, some peanut butter in a little plastic case. She ate it with her fingers.

He promised he would get her out. Promised he would help. But how?

It was hard to remember life outside the darkness. How can you imagine happiness?

She had seen a few movies—once at the theater in the big red seats with the smell of popcorn so overwhelming it made her stomach hurt just to think about it. She played these movies over and over in her mind. Dog movies. Horse movies. Kids-on-the-run movies. She tried to remember what the people in them said, but she couldn't, so she'd make up words. Moms and dads saying, "I love you." She had to make that up.

She listened closely. The creaking floor. Wind against the roof. A scratching, skittering in the walls.

She slept when she could and tried not to dream. Dreams were the worst. Even worse than the darkness.

In the morning, when the light tried to invade, she thought of God. There had to be a God. She had seen people on TV talk about him. Say that he loved her. Knew her name.

She prayed the only way she knew how—in whispers and cries and in a song someone, somewhere, had taught her.

> *Jesus loves me! this I know,*
> *For the Bible tells me so;*
> *Little ones to Him belong,*
> *They are weak but He is strong. . . .*

She clung to the last line like a drowning man to a piece of driftwood. She was weak. Alone. She needed help. Jesus was strong. He would help her because he loved her. He would rescue her.

She had seen pictures of Jesus, with a long, white robe and flowing hair and beard. In the moments before she fell asleep, she imagined him opening the door, a silhouette blocking the light. He would reach down and take her hand, then pick her up and carry her away.

Please, God. Please help me. Please, Jesus. Don't let them hurt me anymore. I won't be bad. I won't try to run away. I won't eat much. Please send someone to help me.

At times she thought she could almost hear him say, "I hear you." But those words were always drowned out by their voices, the yelling and cursing.

It was hard to breathe. She had gotten sick on her first day inside. A headache. Upset stomach.

She leaned back and swallowed. Her tongue stuck to the roof of her mouth. Before she fell asleep again, she looked at the sliver of light at the bottom of the door and said a final prayer. "Please, God, if you're there, I need your help."

CHAPTER 1

◎ *Bryce* ◎

The crack of the bat split the air—one of the best sounds in the world—and the crowd at Coors Field *ooh*ed and *aah*ed. The Chicago Cubs were in the middle of a four-run first inning, and I couldn't believe I was seeing them in person again.

My name's Bryce Timberline. My twin sister, Ashley, doesn't like baseball much—she just comes for the food. My stepdad, Sam, had promised to take us to a game when the Cubs came to town in September, and the place was packed. We had to park a few blocks from the stadium, and Dylan, my little brother, complained about the walk from the minute we got out of the car.

Our stepsister's boyfriend, Randy, finally put Dylan on his shoulders and carried him. Leigh—she's 17 and a senior now—put her arm in Randy's just like Mom did with Sam. I rolled my eyes and hurried ahead, hoping they wouldn't ask to leave the game before the last out.

Sam hadn't said anything about our seats, but I could tell when we went up the thin escalator that we weren't sitting in the cheap ones.

Before we'd sat in the Rockpile in center field, way up in the discount seats you get at the grocery store if you buy $100 worth of food. But I'd never been in this part of the stadium. There were pictures and framed jerseys signed by past players on the walls, plaques celebrating special moments, and even a statue.

But the best part came when Sam ushered us inside a luxury box.

"Wow!" I said. "Sweet."

"Exactly," Ashley said. "A sweet suite."

There was a little kitchen, flat-screen TVs mounted in two corners, a leather couch near the window, and tall barstools along the wall.

"Guy I flew last week offered us this," Sam said. He has a growly voice, like there's gravel in his throat. "I told him how much you were looking forward to the Cubs game, and he said he'd be out of town tonight."

I looked out the big window at the field. A perfect view. We were on the same level with the guys who do play-by-play on TV and radio.

Someone knocked, and three people rolled in steel trays filled with hot dogs, bratwurst, pizza, hamburgers, vegetables, and dip. A cooler taller than Sam held Coca-Cola, Sprite, Dr Pepper, and root beer. Dylan looked inside like he was at a soda museum.

"Do we have to pay for this?" Leigh said.

"I think it's included," Sam said.

Randy grabbed a plate and piled the pizza high.

Outside the window a balcony hung over the field. The 10 seats out there sat in two private rows. I snatched a soda, stacked a bunch of veggies next to a burger, and headed for the front row.

CHAPTER 2

❀ Ashley ❀

I could tell Bryce thought he had died and gone to baseball heaven. His field of dreams. He likes baseball as much as breathing, and if he had to choose, I think he'd rather play or watch baseball.

He remembers our real dad taking him to Cubs games in Chicago. Our real dad died in a plane crash, and in a strange way, that's how Mom and Sam came together. Sam's wife and little daughter were on the same plane. Mom met him at one of the memorial services.

Our real dad had gotten kind of religious on Mom before he died, but she didn't want anything to do with church and the Bible. But after she was married to Sam, who's not a Christian—and neither is

Leigh, his older daughter—something clicked and she started going to church. Bryce and I tagged along, and it wasn't long before we understood about God and what he'd done for us. Now we spend a lot of time trying to convince the people we love the most that God cares for them.

Anyway, when the game started, Bryce was in the front row talking with Randy about batting averages, ERAs, and the play-offs. (Randy plays on the Red Rock High School baseball team, so he knows a lot about that stuff.) Sam sat behind them, his arm around Mom. Dylan had parked himself in front of the cooler.

"You doing that pole thing Tuesday?" Leigh said, crunching cauliflower with ranch dressing. She flipped through the TV channels to a reality show.

"See You at the Pole?" I said.

"Yeah, whatever. You doing that?"

The crowd cheered. Someone had hit a home run. Or struck out. Or maybe a dog had run onto the field and the security guys were chasing it.

See You at the Pole is a nationwide thing where Christian kids gather at the flagpole at their schools to pray and sing.

"Bryce and I probably will."

"Why do you bother?" Leigh said.

At first I thought she was trying to be mean. But the way she said it, the ranch dressing running down her hand, her eyes fixed on the TV, made me think she really didn't understand why anybody would be so . . . radical.

"I think it makes people feel better," she said before I could answer. "If they stand out there in front of everyone, they think God likes them more."

"That's not the way I feel," I said.

She switched to a show where people ate horse-intestine-flavored Popsicles (or something like that). "Then why?"

"Solidarity."

She looked at me like *I* had just eaten a horse intestine.

"It means unity—"

"I know what it means, Ashley. I didn't know you did."

Now she was sounding mean, like an eighth grader shouldn't be using such big words, but she motioned with her cauliflower for me to continue, her eyes glued to the TV again.

"When we stand around that pole and sing and pray, it feels like we're not alone. Even some of the teachers—"

"So it is about a feeling," she said.

"It's more than that. We ask God to forgive us, we pray for the teachers and the administrators, and we pray for our friends who don't know God. . . ."

Leigh turned from the television and stared. "People like me." There were green specks on her tongue from a piece of broccoli.

I shrugged. "I'm just saying. . . ."

She flicked the channel again, and a preacher with perfect hair came on. He held his hands over a big pile of letters and said he was going to pray.

"I'd like to tie this guy to a pole," Leigh said.

CHAPTER 3

◎ *Bryce* ◎

After one of the Cubs hit a home run, I told Randy the pitcher was going to walk the next guy.

When he did, Randy said, "You really know the game."

"Happens a lot," I said. "Pitcher loses concentration after he gives up a dinger. Walks can hurt you as much as home runs in a park like this."

The altitude makes the ball fly out of the park almost as much as the wind makes the ball jump out of Wrigley Field. But as the game wore on, the temperature fell and things changed. The best Cub pitcher was taken out in the sixth inning, even though he had a shutout going (no runs so far for the Rockies). The dreaded walk and a couple of singles by the Rockies and they were back in the game.

I went inside for more food during the seventh-inning stretch. Ashley and Leigh were watching something on TV, making small talk. I'd heard them talking about See You at the Pole earlier. Ashley and I had participated every year since attending Red Rock Middle School. Only this year I wasn't looking forward to it. In the past few weeks I'd been hearing a lot of negative stuff about God. Science class was hard because teachers taught that we basically crawled out of the slime and over millions of years evolved from single-celled organisms to upright humans with cell phones. In history class, God was mentioned only when something bad happened, like a war or a tsunami or an earthquake.

The hardest part of the new year—other than having a principal who wouldn't let us ride our ATVs to school and who put me on the red team and separated me from my sister—was Lynette Jarvis. She was new and beautiful, and she had a chip on her shoulder about God. I almost wanted to hold a cross up before her every time I saw her—like you're supposed to do with vampires. I'd heard she thought I was a Jesus freak, which made me feel good in one sense and bad in another.

I like letting my light shine, but I don't want to shine a blowtorch, and I don't want to come off as a Holy Joe or a Bible Bryce, shoving Jesus on everyone. Our youth leader, Pastor Andy, teaches that you don't have to beat people over the head with the Bible. He says you can be yourself and let God work.

I was thinking about all this when the Rockies staged an incredible comeback. Rockies fans stood and cheered as the bases were loaded in the bottom of the ninth. I root for the Rockies unless they're playing the Cubs. This year Colorado had NO chance at the play-offs, and the Cubs were battling St. Louis for the division lead.

"Can we go now?" Dylan said. He was stuffed with hot dogs and soda, and I was surprised he hadn't fallen asleep.

"We're staying till the end," Sam growled.

My kind of stepdad.

My heart sank as I glanced at the scoreboard. St. Louis had beaten Atlanta. The Cubs had to win to keep pace.

Two outs, two strikes, Rockies down by three, when their catcher slammed a slider into the right-field corner. The Cubs' right fielder played it off the wall but bobbled it before getting it into the infield.

One run in.

Two runs in.

The pinch runner from first was motoring around third when the third-base coach threw up his hands. The runner blew past him. The Cubs' second baseman took the cutoff throw and fired home.

I had a perfect angle to see the ball one-hop the plate, the runner hook slide around the catcher, and the catcher swipe him after he slapped home plate with his left hand and raised a fist with his right.

Tie game.

Blown save.

I shook my head and looked back at Sam. "Looks like extra innings."

Mom looked nervous. As it turned out, she had nothing to worry about. The next pitch was hit high to left field. I thought it was going to curve foul, but it hit the huge yellow pole that runs from the fence to the top of the stadium. They call it the foul pole, but anything that hits it is fair and a home run.

The Rockies fans went wild.

A loss for the Cubs. A full game back of St. Louis.
All because of what happened at the pole.
A bad sign?

CHAPTER 4

✖ Ashley ✖

In Sunday school, Pastor Andy asked how many would be at See You at the Pole on Tuesday. I yawned as I raised my hand. We hadn't gotten back until late, and part of me had wanted to stay in bed.

A couple of kids giggled—as always. Some take church seriously and seem to be there because they want to be, but a lot come just because their parents make them.

I told about my conversation with Leigh but didn't identify her.

Pastor Andy nodded. "To be honest, it can be a show. Just like church. Some people think that if they show up at church on Sunday, they can do anything they want during the week and it won't matter. But one of the signs of a mature Christian is consistency."

"What's that mean?" Bryce said. "That you never sin?"

He shook his head. "I wish we could stop sinning, but that's not going to happen in this life." He drew a dot on the chalkboard, then added a squiggly line that pointed up. "This is the point where you became a believer. Then you make decisions—some good, some bad—and they affect your life. If your faith is genuine, if you really asked God to take control, what you'll see on this graph is a series of decisions that, over time, were more good than bad. The friends you choose, the way you spend your time and money, the things you think about—all this goes into the graph."

"How do you know it's real?" someone said from the back of the room. "How do you know you're not just trying to fool God or your parents?"

"Great question," Pastor Andy said. He read us the list of the fruit of the spirit from Galatians. I'd heard that a billion times—love, joy, peace, and all that—but I'd never really put it together that I had those things inside.

"I can usually be pretty consistent," I said. "You know, be kind to other people, especially here. But at school or at home—" I glanced at Bryce—"it's really hard not to yell at people or get mad at them for stupid stuff."

Pastor Andy nodded again. "That's the true test. You can make us think you're someone you're not when I see you only on Sundays or at youth group. But what happens when you're around the people you spend most of your life with?"

"I think we're all failing that test," Bryce said.

Everybody laughed.

"Ah, but that's where it all comes together," Pastor Andy said. "A lot of people think God grades on a curve. They compare themselves to some bully or evil leader and think they're not as bad, so

God must accept them. But because God's holy, he can't accept anything less than perfection."

"But you said everybody makes mistakes."

"True, but because God is perfect, he can't have anything near him that's imperfect. That's why the angels who rebelled were cast out of heaven. They had one chance to follow God, and one-third of them blew it. End of story."

"So none of us has a chance?" a girl said.

Pastor Andy smiled. "That's the great news. Because of Jesus, we all have a chance to be perfect. Because he was perfect, never sinned, and then died to take the punishment we deserved, when God looks at us, he doesn't see the mistakes. He sees Jesus."

I'd never heard it explained that way, and it gave me a warm feeling. I used to think I had to try hard to please God, do everything right or he was going to be ticked at me and make me stand with my nose to the chalkboard when I got to heaven.

I guess that's what grace is all about, and it made me want to be at the pole on Tuesday morning even more.

CHAPTER 5

☻ *Bryce* ☻

When Dad died, I'd figured he'd gone to heaven because he was such a good father. That made me wonder if I was good enough to get to heaven, and I had wondered how good I needed to be to get to see him again.

But since moving to Colorado and finally understanding that it's not about being good but about accepting Jesus, I've asked God to forgive me.

Still, there are things I don't understand. Like why I mouth off to Mom or do mean stuff to Ashley and Leigh. If God really does live inside me, which is what the Bible says, how could I do those things? Does yelling at my sister mean I'm not a Christian? Did God spill out of me when I did that?

I rode my ATV to the Morrises', a family that has an alpaca farm near us. Mr. Morris had given Ashley and me one of the babies, and we named her Amazing Grace—AG for short. The ATV didn't spook the animals—they just kept chewing and staring at me as I motored up. AG walked to the fence and put her head through to welcome me.

Alpacas are cute, weird-looking animals, but they're gentle. Their fur is soft and really expensive. I couldn't help thinking that Noah must have had his favorite alpacas next to him on the ark.

A car passed, kicking up dust. The alpacas turned their backs and kept eating. Smart animals.

Another car, a dark one, passed going just as fast, and I didn't recognize the people inside. Only a few families live back here, and everybody seems to watch for strangers.

I helped clean the stalls for Mr. Morris and poured fresh feed for AG. When I left, she put her head through the fence again, as if saying good-bye. "Gotta get back for the Cubs game," I said, patting her head.

Her eyes looked sad, and I wondered if that meant we'd lose again. Kind of silly to think an alpaca could predict a baseball game, I know.

I was headed home when the same dark car I had seen earlier swerved around me, leaving me choking on the dust. I pulled over next to the Speed Limit 35 sign and was there only a few seconds when another car barreled out of the dust and came so close that I heard the whine of the tires and felt the wind. The driver swerved or I'd have been squashed.

The car trunk was open and tied with a bungee cord. The trunk lid flopped, and something black hung out of the back.

A body?

CHAPTER 6

❋ Ashley ❋

I was on the phone with my friend Hayley when Leigh asked if I wanted to go with her to Wal-Mart. I about fell out of my chair. I could count on one hand the times she's done something like that. I hung up.

"Why?" I said, tentative.

"Just figured you might want to go," Leigh said, swinging her keys.

Since she got her car on the first day of school and has had her license less than six months, Mom and Sam don't let Leigh drive other kids. But they do allow her to drive Bryce and me to practices and to the store.

We headed toward I-25 with Pikes Peak in the distance. Even though it was still officially summer, patches of snow dotted the top of the 14,000-foot mountain.

"Where's Bryce?" Leigh said as we neared the on-ramp.

I was about to say he was at the alpaca farm when he zoomed along the access road down the hill. "Right there," I said.

Leigh went past the exit and turned around.

Bryce saw us and pulled over. He jumped in the backseat and pointed. "Follow that car."

CHAPTER 7

◎ *Bryce* ◎

I told Leigh what the driver of the car had done, and she looked at Ashley like I was speaking Farsi.

"We're going to Wal-Mart."

"He ran me off the road, almost killed me!" I said. "I have to get his license number."

Leigh pulled out slowly. When we reached the crest, near the ramp to I-25, dust was rising from another dirt road on the other side of the interstate. She crawled up the hill, but by the time we reached the road, the dust had settled.

"Left!" I said.

"Hang on," Leigh said. "This isn't another of your little mysteries, is it?" She made it sound like we were kids with Tinkertoys.

When she began to turn around, I said, "Let me out."

"Wait," Ashley said. "We can go to Wal-Mart as soon as we've seen where that car went."

"You know where this road leads?" Leigh said.

"No," Ashley said.

"Good reason to turn around. Dad would take the car away if I went on some joyride."

I sat forward. "Leigh, just do this one thing for me. I promise I won't ask another favor."

Leigh rolled her eyes. "Right, for at least 24 hours. Okay, I'll go two miles, but then I'm turning around."

She drove slowly on the narrow road. Her car dipped and rocked through washed-out sections, though I couldn't remember rains hard enough to cause all the damage. We went up the hill into pine trees that hugged the road.

"I don't like this," Leigh said, her knuckles white as she gripped the steering wheel.

"Just a little farther," I said.

There weren't many driveways up here, and the ones we saw either went straight up the side of the hill or straight down. Houses had incredible views of Pikes Peak and the front range of mountains.

Suddenly the dark car was back, speeding around a curve and almost hitting us. I caught a glimpse of the driver—beard, mustache, ponytail. Someone sat beside him, but I didn't get a good look.

The car swerved to miss us, and there was too much dust to see the plate. I did notice the trunk was closed.

Leigh said a bad word and slammed on her brakes. Her iPod skittered off the seat and clattered onto the floor, stopping the music.

"Was that them?" Ashley said.

I nodded.

"I'm not following those guys," Leigh said. "I'm going to find a place to turn around."

We snaked our way around the curve and farther up the hill. The road was so narrow that there was no way to turn around. There also weren't any driveways because the hill had become a giant rock. The formation above us was one I had seen from school.

"Always wondered how to get up here," I said.

Leigh gave me a worried look in the mirror.

The road hit a plateau and a circular turnaround with lots of scrub brush and old logs pushed together at the end. We were at the top of the pine trees and the view was pretty, but Leigh didn't seem in a sightseeing mood.

As she turned around, I spotted something in the brush. I asked Leigh to stop, and she growled like a bear. I hopped out, and she threatened to leave without me.

CHAPTER 8

❦ Ashley ❦

I followed Bryce as Leigh hooked up her music again. We hopped over a log and found a pile of garbage bags.

"These were just thrown out," Bryce said.

"How can you tell?"

"If they'd been here awhile, they'd be beaten down by rain and have dirt all over them. Plus, there would be flies."

I'd heard of people finding money thrown alongside the road. I'd also heard of people throwing dogs and cats out in trash bags. Or even worse.

"Should we call the police?" I said.

Bryce shook his head.

"Hurry up!" Leigh yelled.

Bryce ripped open one of the bags, and some stuff spilled out. A big wad of coffee filters was stained red, like a Kool-Aid stain. There were several plastic antifreeze containers, empty duct tape rolls, plastic bottles with the wrappers ripped off, and metal containers that said *lantern fuel* on the side. There was also a strong smell, like ammonia.

Bryce looked at a couple other bags filled with the same type of things, except for one stuffed with broken glass containers.

"Will you two get back here!" Leigh shouted. "There might be snakes out there."

That was enough to send me back to the car.

CHAPTER 9

◉ *Bryce* ◉

Leigh twirled her finger. "Wow, you cracked the case of the serial litterer. Good work, Sherlock."

I already felt stupid.

"Who drinks red coffee?" Ashley said.

"Rudolph," Leigh said, laughing. "How do you think he got that nose?"

I had to force myself not to kick her seat. "I don't think it was coffee. It had a funny smell."

After we got back to my ATV I slammed the door, and Leigh gave me a dirty look. She spun gravel my way and zoomed toward I-25.

I rode back to the house, thinking this was not going to develop into the kind of mysteries Ashley and I had solved in the past few months. Like the road we'd just been on, this seemed like a dead end. Just a couple of guys who drove too fast and threw trash on the side of the road. So what? Probably somebody having a party.

The Cubs won, but I still had an empty feeling the rest of the night. Every time the camera showed the left- or right-field foul pole, I couldn't help thinking of Tuesday and standing around at school, praying and singing with the others. In the past it hadn't bothered me that people made fun of us. But Lynette weighed on me. As much as I didn't want to, I cared what she thought.

Ashley and Leigh came back with a bunch of blue bags with smiley faces—the bags had the smiles. I wanted to talk with Ashley, but I decided against it.

I finally went to my room and pulled out my Bible. Sometimes I just open it and hunt for something to read. I read for a few minutes, but my mind wandered. I tried to pray, but my eyes drooped. I wondered if God heard the prayers of tired teenagers who didn't even know what to pray.

CHAPTER 10

❀ Ashley ❀

Bryce and I had mothballed our mountain bikes—that's a navy term. It's what they do to ships they no longer use. But since our new principal, Mr. Bookman, had banned us from riding our ATVs to school, we pulled the bikes out of retirement.

The first day after we rode them, my legs felt like wet spaghetti. Bryce was in better shape—he'd ridden 200 miles in a bike trip over the summer. Every morning that the bus passed us made me think it would be a lot easier (and less dusty) to just ride it instead of getting to school hot and sweaty.

The phone rang just before we headed out. It was Pastor Andy.

"One of the local radio stations wants someone at the middle school to give a report tomorrow morning. They need someone articulate, and I thought of you or Bryce."

"He's usually better at stuff like this than I am," I said.

"What?" Bryce said.

When I explained, a weird look came over my brother's face—like he'd found more smelly trash bags.

"You do it," he said. "I'm leaving."

Rat! "What do I have to do?"

"Just call and describe what's going on," Pastor Andy said. "They'll be going to callers from several schools in the area. It'll take only a couple of minutes."

It sounded exciting. On the phone with thousands of people listening. It seemed easy. Just tell people what was going on. Kind of like a spiritual correspondent. I've always wondered what it's like being a reporter.

CHAPTER 11

☺ *Bryce* ☺

Riding my bike to school gave me a way to get my frustrations out, pumping as hard as I could, remembering the trip with my friend Jeff.

No way was I going on the radio. I was already confused enough about See You at the Pole. I figured Ashley would chicken out and ask me to fill in at the last minute, which made me want to skip the whole thing.

I chained my bike to the rack and noticed a commotion at the front office. Kids stood in a semicircle, as if watching a fight. As soon as I opened the door, I realized why.

"Let's go into my office and discuss this," our principal said.

"Here is fine," a man said. "To have a religious gathering on school grounds violates the wall of separation."

"Legally, we have to offer the building to any group in the community," Mr. Bookman said. "We could be sued for discrimination if we kicked them out. Now please, let's go inside. . . ."

"I'm not talking about the church that meets here. . . ."

The two finally stepped inside the school office, and I ran into Marion Quidley. As much as I didn't want to encourage her (because I knew she liked me), I asked what was going on.

"Mr. Jarvis is demanding the separation of church and state," she said.

"That's where I've seen him. He's Lynette's dad." I'd seen him drive her to school.

"Right." She turned to me, her face shining like a bright penny on the sidewalk. "You doing the pole thing tomorrow?"

"Why?"

"Looks like Mr. Jarvis is trying to shut it down."

"He can't. They've had tons of court cases already. There's no way they can—"

The front door banged open, and a man in a shiny suit walked through carrying a briefcase. He strode into the office like he owned a front-row seat, and Mr. Jarvis looked up. "Ah, here's my lawyer now."

The door closed and Marion gave me a smirk. "What were you saying about legal cases?"

"What's going on?" someone said. It was a thin kid I'd never seen before. He was short and wore a long-sleeved shirt. He had dark circles under his eyes and his skin was pale, like he was allergic to the sun or something. (Colorado is not a good state for you if you're allergic to the sun.)

Marion told him, and the kid moved toward the sixth-grade wing.

"Who was that?" I said.

"Matt something, I think."

"No last name? I thought you knew everything."

She gave me a look. "He just started this year. If you need to know more, I can—"

"Just kidding," I said.

I stayed as long as I could, but the office remained closed. Maybe the whole pole thing would be canceled.

CHAPTER 12

✖ Ashley ✖

At lunch I had to choose which group to sit with. A few girls from our church youth group always sit together, but I have a hard time not sitting with Hayley and Marion.

Marion eats the weirdest things, and that day she had bean sprouts and tofu. Hayley, who doesn't know that Marion's dad is really sick or that the family has gone through some rough times, asked, "Does your mom pack your lunch or do you?"

"I do. Why?"

"Because your lunch always looks like a commercial for a vitamin store."

Marion laughed and rolled her eyes, but I could tell it hurt her. I try to never make fun of people's clothes or food, but it's hard sometimes.

"Guess you guys will have to meet somewhere else tomorrow morning," Marion said.

"What do you mean?" I said.

"I heard Mr. Bookman is going to announce you can't meet to pray . . . or whatever you do."

"He can't do that."

She ate another spoonful of tofu. "Not what I heard."

My stomach was already doing flips because of the radio interview. What if See You at the Pole was canceled?

"Oh, and tell your brother it's Vega."

"What?"

"The name he asked me about this morning. Matt Vega."

CHAPTER 13

◑ *Bryce* ◑

I was in gym class after lunch when I had my first chance to talk with Lynette. She was spotting someone on the trampoline.

It was scary, because we'd had a few conversations that made me think if I talked to her again she'd bite my head off. But when she glanced at me, she smiled in a peculiar way, like someone caught on the tracks with a train barreling down on them. "Don't blame me."

I looked behind me. "You talking to me?"

"Yeah, don't blame me for what's happening—or not happening—tomorrow."

"I don't know what you're talking about."

"You will."

I was getting changed in the locker room when Mr. Bookman's voice came over the loudspeaker. He pronounced his words crisply, like he was in some kind of contest and won extra money if everyone understood ev-er-y syl-la-ble.

"It's been determined that the See You at the Pole event on school grounds would be unconstitutional."

"Figures," Chuck Burly said as he pulled his shirt on. "If they could rip that plaque down from Jeff Alexander's climbing wall, they can stop kids from praying around the flagpole."

"You'd think with all the bad stuff that goes on in schools," I said, "they'd want kids to pray."

After school Ashley and I rode our ATVs to the Morris farm. Ashley hadn't seen AG for a few days, so she doted on the animal and baby talked to her. Almost made me sick.

When Mr. Morris joined us, I described the car that had nearly hit me and asked if he had seen it on their road lately.

"Haven't seen a beater like that, but I have noticed a lot more traffic than usual. All hours too. Lots of people out here late at night. No idea why."

My cell phone rang. It was Mom. "Bryce, you and Ashley need to come home now. There's an emergency meeting at the church."

CHAPTER 14

✖ Ashley ✖

The parking lot was packed when we got to the church. This meeting wasn't just for kids—it was filled with parents too. There were so many people that we had to move into the sanctuary.

"What are they going to do, arrest our kids for praying?" someone said.

"I think we have it worked out," Pastor Andy said. "As long as this is student led, there's nothing wrong with it. Mr. Bookman was afraid lots of parents and people from the church would be there."

Some parents had red faces and looked like they were about to explode. I had a feeling some of the kids would be transferring to the Christian school soon.

"So it's back on again?" another parent said.

"Our kids don't have to get permission to pray," a man said. "This country was founded on biblical values, and the liberals are doing all they can to take them away."

"They take the Ten Commandments off the walls and then wonder why the kids are cheating on tests!" a lady said.

Pastor Andy calmed everyone down. "I think the kids have a really good opportunity to show God's love to people at the school. Not to shove our rights down people's throats, but to be salt and light."

After the meeting, Pastor Andy handed me a slip of paper. "You're supposed to call this number in the morning just before seven."

CHAPTER 15

◎ *Bryce* ◎

I was nervous on the way to school the next day. Clouds hung over Red Rock like a curtain covering the sun. Everything seemed dingy.

Ashley and I passed the road that leads to the Morris alpaca farm, and three cars were parked by the side of the dirt road. A man with a ponytail was leaning in the driver's-side window, talking with someone. He looked up as we passed, and I noticed dark splotches on his cheeks and forehead. It almost felt like slow motion—him blinking, me studying his face. Who were those people?

At 6:45 we pulled into the parking lot near the flagpole. A television truck with its satellite dish extended was parked near the front of the school. The lawyer I'd seen the day before stood near the entrance with Mr. Jarvis. Mr. Bookman talked on a cell phone, running a hand over his bald spot.

"Most popular See You at the Pole in history," I said.

"I don't like the looks of this," Ashley said. "Where's Pastor Andy?"

"He said he was going to the high school," I said.

I had made up my mind that I'd stand with the others at the pole. Threats have a way of making you see that what you're doing is worthwhile.

Only a couple of kids stood at the pole, like possums in the headlights. They seemed timid, shifting their backpacks from one shoulder to another, no doubt praying more of us would show up.

Ashley gasped. "No!" She fumbled through her backpack, then set it on the ground and riffled through it. "I forgot the phone number."

"Where did you leave it?"

"I thought I put it in here. Wait. Maybe it's still in the pants I was wearing last night."

I grabbed my cell and dialed home. Sam answered, and I heard the radio in the background, tuned to the local Christian station. I imagined him loping up the stairs to Ashley's room, going through her dirty clothes.

"He can't find the pants," I said.

"Tell him to check the laundry room."

Sam's breath got shorter as he ran downstairs.

"Not here either," he said. Then Sam stopped, and I didn't like the silence. "Your mom's doing a load of wash right now."

"Open it up and check!"

Mom's rule is that she doesn't spend time going through the

pockets of our clothes. We have to do that ourselves, or whatever's in there gets ruined.

I heard a lot of commotion, then Sam: "Okay, found the pants. Here's the note."

Ashley wrote down the number, but it was so wet that Sam couldn't tell if one number was a 3 or an 8. Ashley said she'd try both.

"Tell Ashley we'll be listening," Sam said.

CHAPTER 16

❋ Ashley ❋

My hands shook as I dialed. It was 6:55, and a few more kids showed up and stood around with their hands in their pockets.

The first number I tried was the wrong one—an older woman with a cough answered—and I wondered if anything was going to go right today. I changed the 8 to a 3 and dialed again, but the line just rang and rang.

Someone started singing a worship song that Dylan calls the "bouncy music." Bryce joined the group and everyone clapped in time. Well, almost everyone.

Someone finally answered and told me I'd be next on the air. The lights on the satellite truck flashed, and a reporter took his position. My heart pounded.

A song was ending at the station, so I took a deep breath. But they went to a school in Colorado Springs first.

The reporter fiddled with his earpiece and said something to the cameraman. More kids raced to the pole, making at least 20, and the singing got louder. I started to tear up. There was something special about kids taking a stand and those kid voices echoing off the walls of the middle school.

Mr. Bookman came out, talking with the lawyer, shaking his head, and pointing at the pole.

The phone swooshed—a loud, electronic sound pierced my ear, and then I was on.

"And at Red Rock Middle School, we have Ashley on the line," the DJ said. "What grade are you in?"

"Eighth . . . ," I managed. *Please, God, help my mouth work.*

"And what's going on there right now?"

The kids around the pole had joined hands and bowed their heads as Boo Heckler approached. He scrunched up his face at me and said, "What's going on?"

"Hold on," I said.

"Me?" the DJ said.

"No, someone just—"

"They doing a fairy dance around the flagpole or something?" Boo said.

I stepped away from him and was about to start my report when a woman at the radio station said, "Isn't that your school on TV?"

"There is a television truck here, yes."

"Whoa, wait a minute," the DJ said. "Let's back up—"

"Who are you talking to?" Boo said.

"—why don't you start from the beginning?"

The TV camera pointed directly at me.

"Who invited the whole world?" Boo said.

I put my hand over the phone and said, "Go away."

Boo frowned and walked down the hill.

"Is that you on the phone?" the DJ said.

My eyes grew wide, and I waved at the camera. "I guess."

"Cool, this is the first video feed we've ever had on the radio. Now tell us why they're there."

I did the best I could explaining about the upset parent trying to get the event canceled and the lawyer and everything. The DJ seemed really upset. He couldn't believe anyone would try to stop something like See You at the Pole.

I told them how many kids were here and that it was kind of chilly.

The DJ laughed and said, "Why are you out there today, Annette? Why's it important for you to get up early and participate?"

I let the botched name pass and said, "There's a verse in the Bible that says, 'Don't let anyone think less of you because you are young. Be an example to all believers in what you say, in the way you live, in your love, your faith, and your purity.'"

The DJ paused, then said, "You know what I think, Anne? This country needs more people like you, people willing to stand up and be counted. And instead of trying to cancel See You at the Pole, those people at the school ought to be lifting up kids like you, praising you."

Mr. Bookman and the lawyer approached, and the lawyer pushed the camera out of the way and started up the hill.

The DJ told people to tune their TVs to the station. "I hope every one of our listeners will call that school in Red Rock and tell the principal what they think of what's going on there."

As quickly as I had been put on the air, the line went dead and my minute of fame was over.

Boo Heckler stood staring from the bottom of the hill.

CHAPTER 17

☺ *Bryce* ☺

I was standing beside Harris, another kid from our red team, hoping we wouldn't hold hands, when everybody started holding hands. Ashley's friend Elaine was on my other side, and she had the warmest hands in history.

We sang a couple of songs, and then people prayed sentence prayers. It was hard because I knew several kids were there only because their parents made them. When they prayed it was like fingernails on a blackboard—not to judge them, but let's just say their walk and talk didn't match.

The truth is, some people live one way on Sundays and at the pole once a year. Then they are different people the rest of the time. My goal—and it's only a goal—is to be the same whether I'm at church, at school, hanging out with friends, or at a sleepover. Problem is, it's hard not to go along with the crowd.

Every time I looked at Mr. Bookman, I wished we had our old principal, Mr. Forster, back. He would never get in the way of something like this.

Mr. Bookman approached with the lawyer, and Lynette's warning came back to me. I imagined the police zooming up, guns drawn. Antiprayer SWAT teams on the roof. German shepherds barking.

The singing started again. Mr. Bookman was saying something to us, but everyone sang louder.

Then one kid, who looked like he was there to fight and not to pray, said, "You don't belong here! Only kids are supposed to be here."

"That's enough!" Mr. Bookman said. "This is not the place for this type of gathering. You're free to worship as you please, but this is government property."

"We're just praying!" the kid yelled.

I saw the cameraman zooming in, so I stepped between him and Mr. Bookman and the kid walked away.

A few kids hung around, but most left. I found Ashley, who was on the phone with Mom. "She heard the whole thing, Bryce." She turned back to the phone. "You really think I did okay? . . . Well, I don't know about 'fantastic' or 'better than Pastor Andy,' but thanks."

CHAPTER 18

❋ Ashley ❋

I felt bad about the way I had treated Boo. I told myself I had just been nervous about the interview and didn't need any distractions, and Boo was the biggest distraction at the school—except for the lawyer with Mr. Bookman.

Boo slipped into Spanish class behind Mrs. Sanchez as the bell rang. He slunk to his seat, and I tried making eye contact, but he was busy chewing something.

I had seen Boo at our church the past few weeks—not on Sundays, but at strange times—and I wondered what was up. Why was he hanging around?

As soon as class was over, Boo headed for the door, but I cut him off. "I need to talk to you."

He looked at me like I was some kind of lab rat. "You said I should go away," he said, pushing past me.

I said, "Fernando!"—his chosen Spanish name.

He stopped and his neck turned red.

"I'm sorry I blew you off out there. I was stressed because I was on the radio and the TV cameras were going and I just kind of freaked. Okay?"

He turned. "You were on the radio? Mickey and Maury's show?"

That's a radio show in Colorado Springs where they pull stupid stunts and make people eat disgusting things to get concert tickets.

"No, it was one of the Christian stations."

Boo rolled his eyes. "I never listen to those."

"Well, my point is, I was stressed out and didn't mean to be rude."

"You don't have to apologize, Timberline," he said. "Just go back out to your pole and pray."

I couldn't help but think I'd won some great victory on the radio but had lost the war with Boo.

CHAPTER 19

◑ *Bryce* ◑

Kids talked about the See You at the Pole thing in science, and I tried to keep my mouth shut.

Lynette Jarvis had moved to our town from Wyoming, and her dad was the one who had sicced the lawyer on the school. "People can believe what they want to believe," she said, "but when they start pushing it on others, that's bad. I don't believe in God, but I don't push that on other people."

"How is praying around a flagpole pushing religion on you?" I said, unable to stop myself.

"You can do that at home, at church, in a car—anywhere—but

when you come onto public property, like here at school, you should keep your religion to yourself."

"Yeah, it's just a show," someone said. "They want people to think they're good Christians."

"What about freedom of speech?" another said.

Our teacher, Mr. Blunt, raised his head. "Go on."

It was Harris. He's usually pretty quiet. "Well, the way I look at it, if you start telling people they can't talk about the Bible or pray, what's next?"

"You can't yell 'fire' in a crowded theater," Mr. Blunt said, whatever that meant.

"Unless there's a fire," Harris said.

"True."

"I think Christians just want the same rights as everybody else to talk about what's important to them."

"But it's the way they do it," Lynette said, sweeping her long, black hair from her face. "They act like they have all the answers, and if you don't believe like them, you're second-class."

We started talking about evolution, and that really started things going downhill.

"If you believe in evolution, there's no meaning to life," I said. "We just live and die and that's it."

Lynette shook her head. "I believe in evolution, but I choose to make something of my life. I don't have to make up some God to give my life meaning. I don't have to read some book to tell me what to do and not do."

The class went round and round on that one. We got back to whether it was legal for kids to pray in school, and Marion Quidley raised a hand. I knew she didn't like Christianity much from things she'd said and from her wild, space-alien theories.

"I found this on the Internet last night," she said, producing a piece of paper. "Gave a copy to Mr. Bookman this morning. It says that before- or after-school events like the pole thing are okay, and the school can't encourage or discourage participation."

"Could the school be in trouble?" Harris said.

She shrugged. "The report I read says the U.S. Supreme Court has ruled that you can pray out loud or silently anywhere, and if schools try to stop it, they could face a federal lawsuit."

"Hey," Kael Barnes said, "maybe the Christian kids could sue the school and give the money to our sign fund."

Marion smiled at me.

Lynette frowned and shook her head.

CHAPTER 20

❋ Ashley ❋

Bryce had a bunch of homework, so I rode the Ashleymobile toward the Morris farm. It was a breezy, warm afternoon, and it felt good to ride through the pasture, the wind blowing into my helmet. It almost feels like it can clear your brain. It felt even better to ride the ATV since I'd ridden my bike to school the past few days. My legs thanked me as I zoomed across the access road, kicking up red dust.

I came to a turn and slammed on my brakes. A deer crossed the road, stopped, looked at me, twitched its ears, and kept going, disappearing into the tall grass. I looked to my left, and two more were about to jump the fence and follow.

"Come on," I said. "It's okay."

Bambi and his friend didn't trust me, so I took off. I hoped they'd head for the field instead of the main road. I've seen too many deer killed just trying to cross the highway, and it's not pretty.

The clouds hung like a white train. Sunshine lit patches of the grassland. From a distance, it was hard to tell which of the dark patches were shadows and which were little cow ponds.

Most trees near us are huge evergreens that look like they need lights and ornaments. But at the curve in the road is a grove of trees with actual leaves. Bryce and I had built a tree house the summer before, but we'd abandoned it. Teenagers sometimes park in the turnaround and have parties or just talk, so it didn't surprise me to see two cars in the shade. What did surprise me was that one car looked like the one we had seen while riding with Leigh.

I was too far away to see anyone, so I parked behind a big rock at the base of the mountain, left my helmet there, and hurried into the tall grass. The trees were about 200 yards away when I ducked and ran lower to the ground. I stopped to rest with about 50 yards to go, my legs feeling the strain.

The grass waved in the breeze, and I thought of the "amber waves of grain" in the Katharine Lee Bates song "America the Beautiful," which had been inspired by her visit to Pikes Peak. As I got closer to the cars, I forgot all about that song because the car's speakers roared with some head-banging stuff that shook the leaves. I was amazed the windshields weren't cracked from the *boom-boom-boom* of the bass.

I saw the old hideout Bryce and I had made with boards and the ends of crates. I wasn't about to crawl up there, because you never know what will make its home in your hideout when you've been gone a few months. Instead, I inched forward to the beat of the music.

At the edge of the tall grass I laid on my stomach. I was only a few feet from the cars, but the trees hid me well. A mound of dirt lay next to me, like someone had buried an animal. I crept away from the grave—or whatever it was—and focused on the two men outside the older car. One had a red, white, and blue bandanna around his head.

A patriotic rapper.

They were talking and gesturing, but I couldn't hear them.

> *Been backed in a cornuh,*
> *You know I gotta warn ya,*
> *You're gonna get sick,*
> *Have to face the music . . .*

The lyrics sounded like something Dylan would come up with on a bad day in kindergarten. The next song was about a guy who sold drugs to kids, as if that was a good thing.

The guy with the bandanna was dressed in a football jersey, and his jeans were falling off. The other had short hair and was as thin as a cucumber.

Thin Guy pointed toward the road and turned off the radio. My head was still spinning from the music, like it does when you get off one of those amusement-park rides.

"Big money coming," Bandanna Man said. He slapped Thin Guy's hand, and they did a little dance.

A gleaming white car pulled into the turnaround. It looked like a team had washed and waxed every inch of it. Its windows were tinted black, and all I could see was the reflection of the other two guys in wheels that looked like mirrors. The door opened, and two white shoes hit the dusty ground.

"How's it going, boss?" Thin Guy said.

"On schedule, like always," Bandanna Man said.

White Shoes cursed them, and the guys wilted like thirsty flowers in summer heat. He stared at them for several seconds, and I could hear the *drip, drip, drip* of the car's air conditioner.

I raised my head to get a better look, and something creeped me out. Was White Shoes going to hurt them? Was this some kind of drug deal? What had I stumbled onto?

CHAPTER 21

☺ *Bryce* ☺

I was hunkered down with my history homework, wishing I could play Alien Blaster 3, when the phone rang. The caller ID said Private.

"Is this Bryce?" a woman said.

"Yes."

"This is Sylvia Jarvis. I'm Lynette's mother." Her voice was strained, like her vocal cords were being held hostage.

"Oh, hi," I said, stunned.

A pause. "I want you to know I don't appreciate your harassing my daughter in class." She said "harassing" weird, like "harris-ing."

I don't trust people who pronounce it like that. "She's told me some of the things you said, and I don't find them appropriate for science or any other class."

It took me a moment, but I gathered my own vocal cords. "I didn't harass your daughter, Mrs. Jarvis. We were just having a discussion about—"

"She also told me you were one of the children at the flagpole this morning."

"Yeah, but what's that got to do with—?"

"It shows me that what she's saying about you is correct. You're one of those."

I didn't know what she meant by "those," but I was getting tired of being interrupted. I imagined Lynette had to go through this a lot.

"You don't need to know any more than this," she said. "Stop speaking with my daughter. Stop trying to push your beliefs on her. She's uncomfortable with the atmosphere in the school, and the administration will hear about this."

I wasn't exactly happy with the atmosphere at school either, and I thought of a million snappy things I could have said, some having to do with evolution and how the fittest will survive. But she hung up with a loud click.

CHAPTER 22

✖ Ashley ✖

I got an eerie feeling, like I should just stay still, like if they found me something bad might happen.

"Shipment's on its way," White Shoes said.

In the chrome of the wheel I saw Thin Guy rub his hands together. "Money's coming our way."

"If you do your job," White Shoes said. "The shipment will pass through here tomorrow, about two. Meet them at the truck stop. There will be radios in the truck. Take one and keep it in the car so you can talk with each other."

"If the cops—"

"—catch you, you're dead meat. Remember that. Drive the speed limit. Don't do anything stupid."

"What if we have to get gas?" Thin Guy said.

"You won't." He handed them a piece of paper. "Here's a map and the address. You'll be paid when the delivery is made."

"But I thought—"

"When you get there and not before," White Shoes said.

"Okay," Thin Guy said. "That's cool. Do we have to do anything? I mean, do they—?"

"No touching the cargo. Don't even think about it. Just make the delivery and your job's done. Go have a good time."

"You don't have to worry about that, boss," Bandanna Man said.

A multilegged bug crawled onto my arm, and I almost screamed. I flicked it off and looked back at the wheel.

White Shoes was on his toes, staring over the car. "Hear something?"

"Sounded like an animal," Thin Guy said.

As the three moved around the cars, I skittered back into the tall grass and laid on my stomach. I couldn't see the three men, but I could hear them at the edge of the field.

My heart beat like a drum on the sidelines of a football game, and I was sure they could hear it. I tried not to breathe or move or even think. Just lie still.

"I don't see anything," Bandanna Man said.

"Yeah, probably a rabbit," Thin Guy said. "Let's get out of here."

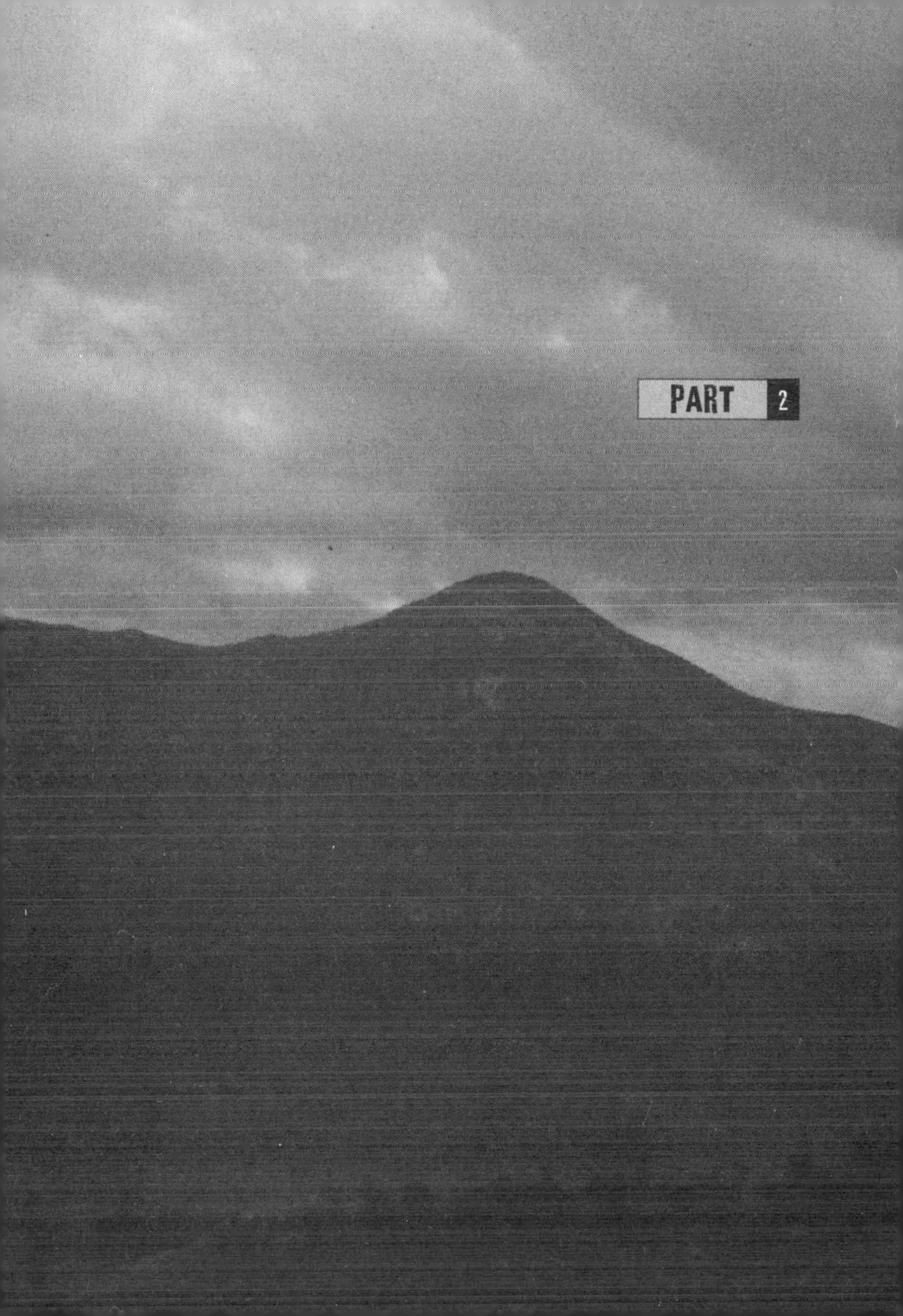

PART 2

She was faint from hunger, more thirsty than she could ever remember. She heard tunes booming through the wall and wished she could have her own music.

Once they had let her have a radio—a tiny one. The voices that came through the speakers were like her friends, and she remembered one station that talked a lot about God and Jesus and the Bible.

But the voices had become scratchy as the batteries ran out, and when she cried for new ones, they took the radio and never gave it back.

She had cried that night because she had lost the only friends she had, other than her brother. She prayed someone would come and rescue her. Maybe someone on the radio could hear her if she called loud enough. But every time she cried, they came again saying mean things, telling her to shut up.

She felt something on the floor humming, whirring, as if they were moving. Were they taking her somewhere? Or was it just her imagination? Was this what hunger and thirst did to your mind?

She pressed herself against the wall and tried to listen for anyone who might help.

CHAPTER 24

◕ *Bryce* ◕

We called the local police station to tell what Ashley had overheard, but the officer we knew wasn't in. I could just see the guy who answered the phone rolling his eyes. *Everybody wants to be a detective,* he must have been thinking.

He connected us to the voice mail of the officer we asked for. "We don't know if it means 2 a.m. or 2 p.m.," I said, "and there are a bunch of truck stops between here and Colorado Springs."

Sometimes grown-ups don't take kids seriously, but a lot of bad things could be avoided if they'd just listen. Of course some kids make things up, but most of us just want to help.

"It's probably happening at two in the morning anyway," Ashley said.

I didn't tell Ashley what Mrs. Jarvis had said. After all, you have to keep some secrets from your sister. But the woman's phone call hung over me like a spider dropping from the ceiling. It's one thing when a kid yells at you and tells you not to do something, but it's different when it's an adult.

I've thought a lot about switching schools. Other kids in our youth group go to a Christian school in Colorado Springs or are homeschooled. I could just see Ashley and me being taught by Mom and observing See You at the Mailbox or See You at the End of the Driveway.

For some reason Mom thinks public school is a good choice for us. Makes me wonder if she knows everything that goes on.

If I went to some other school I probably wouldn't have to put up with all the junk, but I might not have to stand up for God either. At least I'm getting some experience doing that.

I remember hearing once, "If you stand for nothing, you'll fall for anything."

Even though things were uncomfortable at school, I was probably in the best place, at least for right now. If God wanted me to talk to others—even my enemies—about him, even if it was hard, I was willing.

I just wished he hadn't made my enemies so pretty.

CHAPTER 25

✖ Ashley ✖

I woke up in the middle of the night and had to go to the bathroom. Pippin, our white bichon frise, was asleep by my bed and yelped when I stepped on his tail.

When I came back, I had him jump up on the foot of my bed. He's getting a little slower and a lot fatter than Frodo, who can jump about five feet. I glanced at my alarm clock and saw that it was 1:30.

I lay there, imagining someone driving a truck full of drugs from the south and heading for Denver. How many lives would that stuff ruin? How many teenagers would try it just once and get hooked?

Pippin inched up and licked my hand. I turned away from the

clock and tried to get back to sleep. Something kept gnawing at my insides, like a mouse on a hunk of cheese. I turned back. 1:50.

I asked God if he would somehow stop it if something bad was going to happen. *I don't know why you allow drug dealers and thieves and killers, but I pray that you would help the police stop them tonight.*

Next thing I knew my clock beeped and I shut it off. As I got ready for school I flipped on the radio to find out if there had been an overnight drug bust. On my way to the news station, I crossed the Mickey and Maury show. They were just finishing a competition between two listeners for concert tickets. At least five people in the studio were laughing.

"Guess we should ask those kids around the pole to pray for us," Mickey said, giggling. "You see the news about those bozos?"

"Yeah, you'd think kids would be smarter and sleep in," Maury said.

I found the news station and listened for as long as I could stand it—the weather, sports, headlines, lotto numbers, and traffic. No mention of a drug bust.

Maybe the delivery will be this afternoon.

CHAPTER 26

☻ *Bryce* ☻

I tried to stop thinking about Mrs. Jarvis, but it was like someone saying, "Don't think about purple caterpillars." As we rode the bus to school, I watched for her. I figured she'd be holding a sign that said "My daughter is being harassed by Bryce Timberline."

It felt like everyone in school was staring at me as I walked in. I went to my locker and put my lunch away, then looked for the quickest path to first period. I'm Mr. Gminski's student aid for his sixth-grade class.

I've been accused of harassment before, but that proved to be nonsense. This seemed bigger somehow. I guess because Lynette's

mom called and her dad was involved in trying to stop See You at
the Pole.

I figured Lynette would wear a black armband or my name in a
circle with a line through it, but she had on jeans and a short-sleeved
shirt.

I ducked into the bathroom and waited until she passed. When
I finally made it to Mr. Gminski's room, he gave me some papers to
take to the front office. Great, another place I didn't want to be.

I handed the pages to the secretary and tried to get out without
making eye contact with Mr. Bookman. His door was open, and the
room was unusually bright. I couldn't help moving closer—there
were several people behind a camera, the light glinting off Mr. Bookman's bald head.

"We're trying to strike a delicate balance here," he said. "Religious students have a right to express their beliefs, but nonreligious
students also have rights."

"But yesterday you stopped the prayer at the flagpole," the reporter said.

"That was a demonstration," Mr. Bookman said. "I moved in to
stop the kids for their own safety."

"What?" I said, apparently a little too loudly.

The reporter turned to me. Mr. Bookman tried to get his attention, but the guy said, "You were at the pole yesterday morning,
weren't you?"

I nodded.

Mr. Bookman moved toward the door. "You won't be allowed to
speak with students without permission from their parents." He
glared at me as he closed the door.

CHAPTER 27

❀ Ashley ❀

When the final bell rang I hopped on my mountain bike and raced home. Sirens sounded in the distance and I looked at my watch.

2:30.

The sun beat down like it was trying to punish me. Sweat ran down my back and made my shirt sticky. My hands slipped from the handlebars. Some guys think girls don't perspire, but I can tell you they do!

I let the bike fall as I rushed into the house. Mom asked how my day was and I smiled. "Fine." I grabbed a drink of water and headed for the living room. When I was sure Mom wasn't listening,

I snatched up the phone and dialed the police officer Bryce and I knew.

The man at the desk said the officer was on patrol and asked if I wanted to leave a message.

I didn't. "Do you know if there've been any drug arrests or anything like that this afternoon?"

"Not that I'm aware of, miss," the officer said.

I thanked him and hung up as Bryce walked in. Mom hugged him and he endured it, then looked at the caller ID on the phone. "Any calls for me?"

"Not that I know of," she said.

"Good."

I could tell he was upset, but about what?

"Want to ride out to the alpaca farm with me?" he said.

We put on our headsets and I asked what was bugging him.

"Just stuff."

In Bryce-speak, that means, "Leave me alone."

I wished I'd changed out of my sweaty shirt, but riding the ATVs felt cool. I was eager to get to the alpacas. Something peaceful about alpacas helps take your mind off things. There ought to be a bumper sticker that says, "I'd rather be herding alpacas."

As we neared the field I had been through the day before, a dust cloud the size of a Middle Eastern sandstorm rose from the road near the leafy trees. A car shot out the other side and streaked toward the interstate. I pulled up and waited for the dust to settle, then gasped when I saw a rental truck sitting in the open, just about where the guys had met the day before.

Bryce came back to me. "What's up?"

"You don't think that could be the shipment, do you?"

Bryce scanned the road. "One way to find out."

CHAPTER 28

☺ *Bryce* ☺

We rode through the pasture cautiously, and I let Ashley take the lead. She'd been here the day before and knew what kind of people we were dealing with. She pulled to a stop about 100 yards behind the trees. We took off our helmets and listened a few moments. She waved me forward, and we loped through the tall grass to the trees, keeping our eyes on the truck.

When we reached the trees I saw *Haul-It-by-Hand* in small letters on the back of the truck. Is there a way to haul something without using your hands? The license plate was from Texas, but those trucks move people all across the country.

"Was the car that pulled out one you saw yesterday?" I whispered.

She shrugged. "Too much dust. I didn't get a good look."

"Why would they leave a truck full of drugs sitting here in the open?"

"Maybe something spooked them. Or they thought the cops were after them. They were using radios."

"If they're carrying drugs, why would they need a truck that big?" I said. "Even half full, that thing would have to be worth a zillion dollars."

"Maybe they're just waiting and there's someone in the front."

I looked in the side mirrors but couldn't see anything from that angle—plus we were too far away.

"Maybe we should call the police," I said. "From your description, these are rough customers. They're going to do anything they can to keep from getting arrested."

Another out for Ashley. All she had to say was, "Call the police," and I would have pulled out my cell phone right there. But I felt my pocket and realized I didn't have my phone.

"Let's take a closer look, little brother."

"'Little brother'? We're twins."

"I beat you by 57 seconds."

CHAPTER 29

✖ Ashley ✖

No way I wanted to see any of those guys face-to-face. But my curiosity overcame my nerves, and Bryce and I slipped quietly out of the trees and made our way to the truck. A huge metal latch held a big lock. "We're not getting that open without a key," I said.

I wiped sweat from my forehead. The sun was really baking us there in the open—which it can do in Colorado. It can almost feel like a desert, with no humidity and very little rain.

The ground was nothing but red dust, and footprints ran from the truck to some tire marks. We went to the back bumper. No radio. No one on a walkie-talkie.

Bryce looked down the right side of the truck, me the left. I could see the steering wheel and front seat through the side mirror. I stepped away and kept my eye on the mirror—something moved in the other mirror! My heart skipped a beat before I realized it was Bryce.

"Front's empty," he called.

So we didn't have to whisper. The window was down on the driver's side, and I jumped onto the running board. Bryce opened the passenger door and climbed in. There was a bag of potato chips on the seat and crumbs on the floor. Candy bar wrappers stuffed the ashtray, along with a bunch of cigarette butts. An empty Diet Coke can sat in the cup holder.

"Must be trying to cut calories," Bryce said.

We looked for the key, but in the glove compartment Bryce only found a manual. I pulled down the driver's-side visor and a key fell. I put it in the ignition and it fit. I stuffed it into my pocket.

"Is that a coyote yipping?" I got out and peered into the field.

We closed both doors, and I heard the yipping again but muffled. I listened closely as the wind picked up and blew a hot blast in my face.

The sound wasn't coming from the field. It was coming from inside the truck.

CHAPTER 30

☺ *Bryce* ☺

It didn't sound like a coyote to me. It sounded human.
The hair on the back of my neck rose as I heard a bang from inside
the truck. I stood on the wheel and put my ear to the side. I heard
faint movement, like mice scurrying in the walls of an old house.

I banged on the side. "Hey!"

"Could there be animals in there?" Ashley said.

"Maybe I'm hearing things," I said.

I sure was. Crying. A baby wailing.

"*¡Socorro!*" someone screamed from inside.

I could barely hear it.

"Someone's inside, Ash!"

The pounding became more intense, and I realized it wasn't just one or two people, but a dozen or more. *"¡Por favor, ayúdenos¡ No podemos respirar. ¡Abra la puerta¡"*

I ran to the back. "We have to get them out!"

Ashley examined the lock. "We have to find the key to this thing."

"They don't speak English—tell them we're going to get them out."

She scrunched up her face, obviously trying to remember what she'd learned. "Um . . . *vamos* a . . . um . . . *atacarlos.*"

No sound from inside.

The back door wasn't just locked, but it also looked airtight. If true, it had to be hot inside and hard to breathe. The people wouldn't last long with the truck sitting in the sun.

"I have to get to a phone," I yelled as I ran toward my ATV. "Look for the key to that lock. I'll find something to cut it off in case you don't."

CHAPTER 31

❈ Ashley ❈

I grabbed a flashlight from the truck cab and crawled to the grate. I banged a few dents in the thing, but there was no way it was coming off without a screwdriver.

I wondered why the people inside hadn't called out when we first got there. What were they afraid of? And why were they locked in the truck in the first place?

I wanted to say, "I'm trying to get you out," but my Spanish was getting all mixed up in my head. *"Trato . . . la puerta . . . atacar."*

No response.

I looked for the key in the truck, but there was nothing. A child cried through the vent.

"¡Ayúdenos! ¡Ayúdenos!" the people yelled. I figured it meant "Help us!" or something, but there was nothing more I could do. I tried to tell them help was on the way, then buried my face in one arm and cried.

I heard the crunch of tires in dirt, and a cloud of dust wafted over me. The car was back.

CHAPTER 32

☺ *Bryce* ☺

I've never driven my ATV that fast. I pushed the accelerator as hard as it would go and just held it there, leaning as far as I could this way and that to keep my balance as I maneuvered around mounds and ruts. Soon I was out of the grass and onto the road that led to the Morris farm. Their big dog, Buck, ran along the fence, barking at me all the way to the barn.

My heart sank to find the Morrises gone. Mr. Morris has a phone on the wall of the barn, and I punched the speaker and dialed 911. At the same time, I looked for the hacksaw I had seen hanging from the tool bench.

"Emergency 911."

I told the woman what we'd found, and she asked the name of the road. I couldn't remember it.

"How many people are in the truck?"

"I don't know. A bunch."

"You haven't seen them?"

"We can hear them. They're speaking Spanish."

"Do you need an ambulance?"

"Probably. In case somebody's hurt or passed out from the heat or lack of air."

"All right, son, you did a good thing."

I grabbed a screwdriver, the hacksaw, and what I thought was a bolt cutter. It seemed like hours, but a quick glance at my watch told me I'd been gone only a few minutes.

I jammed the accelerator again as I adjusted my helmet with my free hand. Buck raced me to the front gate, and I was soon headed back to the truck. There was so much energy pumping through my body, I felt like I could fly back.

I cut through the field, which saved me a couple of minutes, and zoomed toward the trees. When I noticed a car near the truck I slid to a stop.

CHAPTER 33

✖ Ashley ✖

I froze behind a tire as the guys talked.

Their car radio blasted the same music I had heard the day before, pumping and booming so loud that I thought the car should bounce. The music stopped and the doors opened. I listened for a siren, hoping Bryce had made it to a phone.

"You're gonna screw this up if you don't stop getting spooked," Thin Guy said. "You want us to lose the money?"

"I don't want to go to jail," Bandanna Man said.

"Just drive the truck. No one's sending you to jail."

"I heard a siren, and I thought they were after us."

The people in the truck screamed and banged. The baby's wails cut to my heart. Bandanna Man moved toward the truck. I had to do something. If I had time I could have let air out of the tires. I could run to the front and block the vehicle with my body, but I had no doubt these guys would flatten me like a tortilla shell.

Bandanna Man jumped inside. I thought he might say, "Someone's been in here," like in the story of the Three Bears, but there were so many food wrappers and crumbs, he must not have noticed.

"Hey, where are the keys?" he said.

Thin Guy stomped to the truck. "Did you take them with you?"

"No, I stashed them behind the visor when I heard the siren."

Thin Guy cursed, then yelled at the people in the back to be quiet. The men went back to their car.

I spotted Bryce kneeling in the tall weeds and held up the key, and he waved me over. I crept toward the back of the truck.

"I'm telling you, it's not here!" Bandanna Man said. "I swear I left it in the truck. Somebody must have taken it."

"Right, a squirrel?"

Bryce put up a hand, signaling me to wait.

"Maybe you threw it in the back," Thin Guy said. He was bending over the seat.

This was my chance.

CHAPTER 34

☺ *Bryce* ☺

I waved frantically, but Ashley hesitated. Finally, she raced toward me, clouds of dust rising behind her. I always brag about being the better athlete, but she's pretty fast.

The guy with the bandanna walked toward the truck.

Come on, Ashley!

The guy tossed a cigarette on the ground and looked up. "Hey! There's a kid! Hey!"

I left the tools in the weeds and ran to my ATV.

"Come here!" the guy yelled.

I zoomed onto the dirt and did a spin. Ashley jumped on her ATV and had it started as I spun toward her. We hit the tall grass, and I looked back to see the men running toward us, flailing and raising their fists.

We raced through the grass and went down a dip, then up to a plateau.

Ashley pulled beside me. "No way they can follow us, right?" she said.

I looked back and gasped as their car skirted the trees and barreled through the field, bouncing and shaking through ruts. Both men had their hands against the roof of the car.

"Come on!" I said.

I retreated to the edge of the plateau and down through some serious rocks, Ashley right behind me. A little cow pond lay at the bottom of the pasture. If only I could lure them into that!

The car stopped at the plateau. I sat there, hoping to draw them like a stray dog with a hot dog. But the car backed up, then turned around. Ashley and I followed, and when we reached the plateau, the car was engulfed in a dusty fog and headed for the interstate. I felt bad about leaving the people in the truck, but we hadn't had a choice. We could have been no help to the people if those guys got the key back.

I grabbed the tools I'd stashed in the weeds, and we headed back. The people were banging and shouting, and I knew we had to act fast.

CHAPTER 35

❀ Ashley ❀

Still no sirens. I wondered if Bryce had given 911 the wrong directions.

We tried the bolt cutter but couldn't get it to work. Bryce tried the hacksaw, but the lock was so thick it would have taken us a couple of weeks to cut through it. He tried prying the latch where the lock was fastened.

"Está bien," I said. *"Ayuda . . ."* And then I remembered I had said *atacarlos* earlier instead of *ayuda.* One means "help," and the other means "attack."

I leaned against the truck and did the only thing I could. I prayed.

It's one thing to hold hands around a flagpole and pray, but it's a lot different when people are going to die if you don't help them. I asked God to save these people.

When I heard the siren I ran, waving and screaming. A sheriff's cruiser, going way too slow, finally pulled beside the truck, but it took him a minute to get out—talking on his radio, I guess.

When he opened the door we spilled the story.

Concern washed over his face. The only sound was the clicking of the lights on top of his car. No screams. No cries for help.

"Hurry!" I said.

CHAPTER 36

☾ *Bryce* ☾

When the officer finally heard the people, it sounded like they were running out of energy. He said something in Spanish and studied the lock, then took the bolt cutter and applied it to the end. The muscles in his arms strained, and his face turned red. With a grunt, he succeeded in snapping the metal. He yanked off the lock and opened the door.

People lay on the floor, men with their shirts off, some passed out. Others squinted and covered their eyes. I reached to help a woman down, but someone pushed her and she fell.

"*¡Alto! ¡Alto¡*" the officer yelled, but they kept bounding out, gasping.

"*¡Agua, por favor!*"

I knew what that meant and ran back to my ATV for my water bottle.

The officer called for help on his radio. He managed to get the people under control and had them sit in the shade.

"They from Mexico?" Ashley said.

"Have to be," I said. "That must have been what those guys were talking about when they mentioned the 'shipment.'"

Ashley shook her head. "How could they treat people this way?"

"You'd have to really want to come to America to go through this," I said. The truck smelled like a cattle car, and the people cried and hugged each other.

At the front of the truck, wooden, boxlike cartons on either side looked like places where people put their valuables. You could see through several slats, and I thought I saw something move.

Ashley jumped up into the truck.

CHAPTER 37

Ashley

The stench was unbelievable. Several people had passed out and had to be dragged out. When I got to the front, I lifted a handle revealing the inside of the crate. A girl lay with her eyes closed, sweat glistening. I feared she might be dead and yelled for Bryce. He helped me carry her outside.

A woman screamed, *"¡Mi hija!"* and tried to stand, reaching toward the child. "Maria!"

The girl's eyes fluttered and she stared at me. *"¿Eres un ángel?"*

"No, *soy* Ashley."

The group gathered the girl in, and the officer asked Bryce and

me to move back to our ATVs. Several other police cars arrived, one
with a huge supply of water. A few minutes later an ambulance arrived and paramedics examined people, starting with Maria.

A car passed and Bryce waved at the kid in the back. The kid
didn't wave back.

"Who's that?" I said.

"Sixth grader. The one Marion Quidley told you about. His
name's Matt."

Soon three white vans were filled with the people. Several looked
our way and waved. Some said, *"Muchísimas gracias."*

The officer took our names and the little information we knew
about the two guys. Neither of us could tell him the license number
of their car.

"You saved a bunch of lives today," he said. "Thirty-seven, counting the little girl. They paid a lot of money and were told they were
being taken to Denver. Who knows where they'd go from there?"

I couldn't imagine saving for a long time and taking the chance to
come to our country and then almost dying.

A news van appeared on the road above us.

The officer smiled. "They're going to want to talk to you."

But Bryce and I climbed on our ATVs and rode away.

CHAPTER 38

☺ *Bryce* ☺

It wasn't that Ashley and I were so humble we wouldn't have enjoyed being on the news. But Sam had warned us that any kind of publicity could lead newspeople to him, which would be bad. He used to be in a special military unit that fights terrorists, and somehow one of the main terror guys found him. That's why the plane my dad was on was blown up—the terrorists thought Sam was on it.

Later Ashley and I watched the news coverage as the reporter, a young guy with moussed hair, stood before an empty truck and

tried to make it sound interesting. They showed the illegal aliens being taken to a holding facility. Ashley pointed the little girl out.

Mom put a hand over her mouth. "I can't believe you two found
them. What would have happened if you hadn't shown up?"

I hated to even think of that. "They might have made it to Denver," I said.

"But they also all could have died," Ashley said.

The reporter knelt in the dirt. "Two young teenagers spotted this
truck and called the authorities. Without their bravery and quick ac-
tion, this story could have ended in tragedy. Late this evening, those
in the back of the truck say they have a message for those two kids. It
is simply *gracias*."

I could hardly stop thinking of what might have happened if those
people hadn't gotten out.

Once in bed, I fought sleep, afraid I'd have nightmares. And
something else bugged me. It was seeing Matt Vega in the car. His
dad didn't even stop—if that was his dad driving. In a small town
like Red Rock, everybody wants to know what's going on, and they
didn't even slow down.

There weren't that many houses past the Morris farm, and I wondered where Matt lived. Finally I crept down to the kitchen and
looked in the phone book. There were no Vegas in the directory.
I logged on to the Internet and punched in the name and our zip
code into a phone directory.

Nothing came up.

CHAPTER 39

❀ Ashley ❀

At school the next day it seemed everyone had an opinion about who had called the police about the aliens. Most thought it was high schoolers. It wasn't easy, but I just let everyone talk.

In Spanish a debate started about whether or not the people should be sent back to their country.

"If they have enough money and want to risk their lives to get here, they ought to be able to stay," someone said.

"Not if they're doing it illegally," another said. "They take jobs from Americans who don't have work."

"They do the jobs none of us want to do."

"If you let those people in, terrorists will get in the same way. The border ought to be shut. Plus, they don't even speak our language. If you want to come here, the least you can do is learn to speak English."

Hayley raised her hand. "My great-grandfather came here from Europe and didn't know any English. He worked really hard and tried to learn it, but my dad said he always talked kind of funny."

"Yeah, but at least he tried to learn it. The people in that truck probably would have stayed here their whole lives and never learned 'hello' and 'good-bye.'"

My classmates made it sound like the people in the truck were just a nuisance, like mice in your attic.

I finally said, "One thing yesterday proved was how dangerous it is when someone puts their life in the hands of greedy people. And we can't forget that those were real people, just like you and me, with hopes and dreams and a desire for a better life."

I hadn't planned on a speech—it just spilled out. The class got quiet, and I wondered if people had figured out that Bryce and I had been the ones to find the truck.

Cindy Lopez smiled at me. She has beautiful brown eyes and a complexion I'd pay for.

"How did your family get here?" I said.

"My father applied to come to this country before I was born," she said. "He waited many years and made sure everything was legal."

Boo Heckler shook his head. He usually doesn't pay much attention. Sometimes he snores.

"Yes, Fernando?" Mrs. Sanchez said. "Want to join the discussion?"

Boo sneered at her. "I don't know why you people are sticking up for these taco eaters. They just run down neighborhoods and take over with all their kids. All these Holy Joes who hold hands around the flagpole should get out there and do something about that."

CHAPTER 40

☺ *Bryce* ☺

Since it was a nice day, at lunchtime a lot of kids moved outside to eat. I took a quick glance around the cafeteria and noticed Matt on the stairs leading to the band room.

His face was long and his skin pasty. There were dark circles under his eyes, and his teeth had lots of room to grow. His crumpled lunch bag looked like it had been used 500 days in a row, and I could see the outline of half a sandwich.

"Hey," I said, waving and smiling, unable to think of anything more original.

Matt looked like I had caught him stealing from the kitchen. He scooted back toward the wall. His shoes were dirty and the laces frayed. The cuffs of his pants were ragged. I'd seen him in the same outfit the day before—in fact, I'd never seen him in anything but this outfit.

"How's it going?" I said.

"What do you want?" he said. Some sixth graders think eighth graders just want to beat them up or steal their lunch money.

"I saw you yesterday, going past the truck."

"You and your sister were the ones . . ." He looked at the floor like he was going for his degree in carpeting.

I leaned against the wall. "Can I ask you something?"

"Why?" Matt said. "You don't even know me."

"How am I supposed to know you if I never talk to you?"

That made him look up. "What do you want?" he said. His lips were chapped. He looked almost as bad as the people who got out of that truck.

I slid down the wall and sat on the step. "Where do you live?"

"Out that road you were on. Where do you live?"

I told him. "You guys didn't even slow down yesterday. Weren't you curious?"

Matt shrugged. "Guess my dad figured it was none of our business."

He still seemed uncomfortable, so I changed the subject. "My dad flies airplanes."

He lifted his eyebrows. "Really?"

"Yeah. I should see if he'd take you up for a ride sometime."

Matt's mouth dropped open. "You mean it? You really think he'd . . ." He focused on the floor again.

I leaned forward. "Matt, is something wrong?"

He didn't move.

"I saw you at that pole thing," he said finally.

I nodded. "Yep. Are you a Christian, Matt?"

He squinted. "Guess so."

When kids came out of the band room, Matt and I moved away from the wall.

"I gotta go," Matt said, grabbing what was left of his lunch. He walked away, taking small, seemingly painful steps.

CHAPTER 41

❋ Ashley ❋

I sat with Cindy Lopez at lunch, and nobody wanted to bring up what we were all thinking. I could only imagine how she felt.

Marion Quidley came in late and devoured her eggplant sandwich. When Cindy left, I told Marion what had happened in Spanish and she winced. "After being sent to juvenile hall over the summer, Boo seems worse."

"I thought he'd gotten a little better," I said. I felt a twinge in my stomach. If Boo ever found out Bryce and I were the ones who had figured out he was destroying property around town, we were in big trouble.

"Plus with all the stuff going on with his family . . . ," Marion said.

"What stuff?"

Marion knew just about everything going on in Red Rock, and if she didn't, she had a theory. "I have a friend who knows the family," she began. "The mom and dad are having trouble."

"Divorce?"

She nodded. "My friend said they were getting counseling at some church," she said, like it was the worst thing in the world. "They're renting that farmhouse, if you can call it that, on the back side of Kangaroo Rock. Boo has an older brother in the military. There's a younger sister, too."

"A lot of kids have parents who are having trouble," I said. "They're not all mean like Boo."

"But something bad happened before they moved here. I don't know what, but I have my suspicions."

"What?"

"Something to do with Boo. His mom and dad fight a lot about him or something he did."

"Where did they move from?"

Marion shrugged. "I've never heard him say anything about where they lived, and I don't make a habit of conversing with him."

CHAPTER 42

☾ *Bryce* ☾

Ashley and I rode out to Kangaroo Rock after dinner. It's a good half hour ATV drive through backcountry and intense pine trees. You can actually ride out onto the rock, but it's scary.

Kangaroo Rock sits high above the town and looks like, well, a kangaroo. Of course you can't see its pouch or snout and whiskers, but it's in the general shape of a kangaroo. It even has a tail, just a nub that sticks up over the trees behind the rock.

Boo Heckler had been a burr under our saddles for two years, and I didn't really care why he was so mean. Ashley, on the other hand, held out hope that he could change.

We parked and climbed the backside of the kangaroo. Ashley sat in the middle of a rock archway—what they call the eye of the kangaroo. Lots of people climb here and take pictures, because Pikes Peak and the Front Range are perfectly framed in the background. I'd like to build a house here one day, but I doubt the kangaroo lovers would permit it.

We used high-powered binoculars to look down at Boo's house. We could have driven over there, but taking the ATVs anywhere near Boo was a bad idea.

Ashley scanned the area. "Boo's outside working on a car."

"So? What are you looking for?"

"I don't know, maybe a clue to his past." She set the binoculars down. "You know, I was hoping you'd take the lead on this."

"On what?"

"Trying to reach a guy. A girl shouldn't do it. At least that's what Pastor Andy says."

"Yeah, if romantic feelings get in the way. You got feelings for Boo?"

"Hardly, but he's so starved for attention, he could get interested in me just because I give him the time of day. Last thing I want is him asking me to some school dance."

"You'd make a cute couple."

She rolled her eyes.

"Seriously, I can see him taking you to dinner, wrestling a cow, or clubbing a fish."

"Stop."

"Ashley Heckler. Has a ring, doesn't it?"

She shoved me and moved to the other side of the kangaroo.

I peered down at Boo's house. An old car sat behind the barn, which was in as bad a shape as the car. Boo was bent over the engine. He'd stand back, look at the engine, go back under the hood, move to the driver's side and try to start it, then get back out and kick the side. It was kind of funny.

"At least we know what he's interested in," I said.

Ashley didn't answer.

I turned the binoculars toward the red rocks behind our house, and a dust cloud rose in the distance. It was coming from the road to the alpaca farm. Two cars turned onto the access road and headed for the interstate.

CHAPTER 43

✽ Ashley ✽

The sun was setting when we got home. Pastor Andy called and told me, "There's a push to bring a lawsuit against the middle school for what they did. Some say your rights were violated when they made you stop, and they need to be taught a lesson."

I got that sick feeling. "Enough people hate Christians around here as it is. I can't imagine how they'll treat us if this happens."

"We need to hear your viewpoint at a meeting tomorrow," Pastor Andy said. "Bring your brother too."

CHAPTER 44

☻ *Bryce* ☻

Mr. Gminski passed out a quiz the next morning, then asked me to keep an eye on the class and collect the papers when everyone was finished. He stepped out, leaving a reading assignment on the board in case he was late returning.

After I picked up the quizzes, the sixth graders opened their books.

"Before you start your reading," I said, "I'm wondering if anyone knows Matt Vega."

They just stared, some with their mouths open.

A short kid in the back raised his hand, which made me feel like a teacher. "You talking about Ghost?"

A girl in front of him turned. "I know who you're talking about. White as flour and thin as a potato chip."

It was interesting that only one kid seemed to know his name, but as soon as Ghost was mentioned, everybody knew who they were talking about. They described where he hung around, how he always came to school in a dirt-splattered car, and someone said he had never dressed for gym class. "Maybe he's got some kind of blood disorder," someone said.

"Or ghosts might not like tumbling."

The others laughed.

Another boy raised his hand. "I think he's sick. I saw him at the dollar store the other day with his mom. I guess it was his mom. Anyway, they were carrying boxes full of cough syrup."

Strange.

"Does he have any friends?"

A cute redheaded girl, with freckles and glasses that made her look like a bookworm, said, "I saw him talking to Ernie once in the lunchroom."

I asked who Ernie was. They said he was a chess clubber who loved science and model rockets.

While they were reading I looked in Mr. Gminski's grade book. He had another sixth-grade class during third period. I scanned the names until I came to *Ernie Spier.*

CHAPTER 45

✖ Ashley ✖

Bryce didn't want to go to the church meeting that night. "The parents will never listen to me," he said. "If you want to waste your time on something that's already decided, go ahead." He said he was going to visit a ghost house.

Mom drove me to church, and the lot was packed again. Even the cars appeared to be parked angrily. People had apparently zoomed up to the building and jumped out.

Pastor Andy was at the pulpit when I sat down. "So my approach," he was saying, "in a nutshell, is to ask how Jesus would handle this. Would he file a lawsuit? Or would he try to love the people in the administration and show them kindness and forgiveness?"

A man in a suit, who looked like he had stopped in on his way home from work, moved toward a microphone in the aisle. "I like you, Andy, but I disagree. Christians have just as much right to free speech as the next person, and we can't let that right be challenged. If we don't fight for our rights, who will?"

Next a mom wept as she talked about how she remembered saying grace in a public school before lunch every day. She didn't say whether she favored suing the school, but everyone was nodding as if to encourage her.

Another man said we should be careful about suing because the money for the lawsuit would come from taxpayers. Another said it was the principle that we needed to remember, and I thought, *No, it's the* principal.

Finally Pastor Andy said, "I think we should hear from one of the students. Come on up, Ashley."

CHAPTER 46

☽ *Bryce* ☾

I rode past the Morris farm and a few other houses. The road got dustier and dustier the farther I rode, and there were ruts big enough to bury an elephant.

Wire fences ran by the road, and I saw horses, alpacas, and sheep grazing. It almost felt like another world, and the farther I went, the more the mountain next to me blocked Pikes Peak, the Front Range, and even the sun. A grove of pine trees made things way too shady and spooky.

The road led straight up a hill, turned left, and wound into flat country. I slowed at several driveways, looking for the car.

A lot of the houses were log cabins with hot tubs right behind them. One place looked like the cover of a magazine, with a wrap-around porch, big log pillars, and a putting green in the front yard.

I drove for half an hour without coming upon another vehicle, strange because I was back here to see where all the traffic was coming from.

I investigated every road and every turnoff, but I couldn't find one mailbox that said *Vega* or one driveway with a car that looked like the ones that had almost run me off the road.

CHAPTER 47

✖ Ashley ✖

I've heard that the number one fear of most people is speaking in front of a group. Supposedly the fear of death is actually second to that.

I suffered from fears one and two. I was scared to death. I tried not to say anything dumb, but the first thing out of my mouth was "Um . . ." Our speech teacher, Mr. Gminski, tries to keep us from ever saying *uh* or *um.*

I took a deep breath. "Trying to keep us from praying at school is dumb, but I honestly think Mr. Bookman was just scared and did something on impulse. He's new, and I think once he knows the truth about what you can and can't do, he'll follow it."

I sensed a lot of people disagreed, but when I faced Pastor Andy he was smiling.

"Kids have to learn to live out their faith, and if parents . . . well, I know people are upset, but it's going to make it harder for us to talk about our faith and share what's really important with teachers and students if we do this."

"Why do you say that?" a man said, not in a mean way, but like he was just curious.

"Kids are pretty much open to God and Jesus or even the Bible," I said. "Where they get stuck is with people. They freak out when Christians don't live what they believe. If we sue the school, we may win a legal battle, but it feels like we'll lose a chance to tell people what's really important."

CHAPTER 48

☺ *Bryce* ☺

Monday morning I found a yearbook picture of Ernie Spier with his hair slicked to one side. He wasn't smiling. He wore thick glasses and had ears about two sizes too big.

I watched as kids jumped off their buses. Ernie was easy to spot. I called to him, and he pushed his glasses up and squinted. An eighth grader talking to a sixth grader was like the U.S. president chatting with a pizza delivery guy.

"I do something wrong?" he said.

"No, I just want to talk about Matt Vega."

Ernie seemed deep in thought. "Ghost? I don't know him that well. I've just talked with him a few times."

"Know where he lives?"

He shook his head. "We never talked about it. Doesn't ride the bus. I think his dad or somebody drives him."

"He ever talk about hobbies?"

Again, he shook his head. "Well, he had a sketch pad once."

"What did he draw?"

"Birds and stuff. Animals. Dragons and snakes with big fangs. Why don't you just talk to him?"

"I talked to him once but . . ."

"He doesn't say much, right?"

The bell rang and Ernie moved toward the doors.

"Do you know what his dad does? Or his mom? Does he live with both of them?"

Ernie bit his cheek. "He said something about having a little sister. I asked him what grade she was in, but he said she doesn't go to school."

"Must be too young."

He shrugged, then opened the door. "You were one of those kids around the flagpole the other day, weren't you?"

I nodded.

"You guys really going to sue the school?"

It was my turn to shrug. I followed him inside and saw Coach Baldwin. I asked if he knew Matt and he nodded. "There a reason he doesn't dress for gym?"

Coach Baldwin gave me a look like it was none of my business. "Brought a note from home. That's all I know."

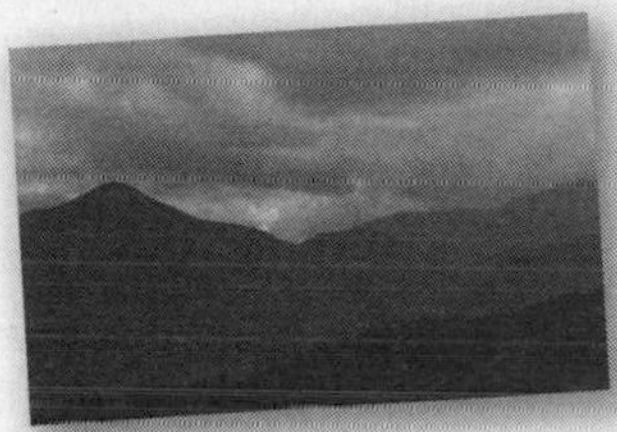

CHAPTER 49

Ashley

After school, I rode my bike over to Juicy Pages, the business our former principal started. Mr. Forster and his wife rented an old library and fixed it up, and now it's a nice bookstore and juice bar.

I had worried the business might not make it, but every time I passed there were cars parked out front.

Mr. Forster was helping a customer. I looked over their "Classic Reads for Kids" and found a bunch I'd already read. Just looking at a book, seeing the cover, and picking it up gives me a good feeling. It's almost like the characters are trapped inside, and opening it makes them come alive.

Anne of Green Gables was a favorite. I picked up *The Lion, the Witch and the Wardrobe* and remembered our real dad reading it to us one winter.

The front door jingled, and I looked through the shelves to see Boo Heckler. He walked up to Mr. Forster, now at the cash register. Boo's arms hung low and reminded me of my first trip to the primate zoo. That seems mean, but it's true. I don't believe in evolution, but if I did, Boo was the missing link.

"Can I get my drink?" Boo said.

Mr. Forster headed for the juice machine. "Sure, what'll it be this week, Aaron?"

"That berry thing with the extra power deal."

"Sure you don't want to try something else? You have that every time."

"No, if I like something, I stick with it."

Boo was getting one drink a week for a year because he'd helped Mr. Forster out of a jam. From the way Mr. Forster talked and smiled, it seemed he liked Boo.

"Read the book I gave you?" Mr. Forster said.

Boo twirled a rack of postcards. "Some of it."

"What did you think?"

"It's okay, I guess. I'd rather watch a movie."

"Movies are good, but they can never help you get into a story the way a book can. Reading exercises the mind."

"You sound like Mrs. Ferguson."

Mr. Forster laughed as he stuck the metal cup under the grinder. "I'll make you a deal, Aaron. You finish that book by next week and I'll give you a coupon for a free rental at the video store."

I wished I could get in on that deal. Why was Boo so special?

"Ashley?" Mr. Forster said. "I didn't know you were here."

Boo stared at me, grabbed his drink, then ambled out like he had just picked a fresh batch of bananas.

Mr. Forster offered me a free drink, and I told him he'd go out of business if he didn't quit giving stuff away. "All part of getting started," he said.

We talked about the See You at the Pole controversy, and Mr. Forster said he hoped it wouldn't cost the district a lot of money. I agreed.

"Do you know anything about Aaron's background?" I said.

"Not a lot, but he's been through some tough times."

"I don't mean going to the juvenile detention center. I meant—"

"I know, before he ever came to Red Rock."

"What happened?"

"I'm not sure, but from the meetings I had with his parents, I know they're having problems. That's always tough on a kid Aaron's age."

"Where did they come from?"

"Texas, I think. Mr. Heckler worked at an oil refinery. They moved here after something happened."

"An explosion or something?"

Mr. Forster shook his head. "I don't think so. But it affected the whole family.

"Any idea where in Texas the Hecklers came from?"

He ground my drink into a red froth. "I think it started with an *L*."

CHAPTER 50

☻ *Bryce* ☻

After school I went to unhook my bike. I fiddled with the lock and it jammed. When I finally got it unhooked, I noticed someone in the upper parking lot by the door. Most everyone had either gotten on a bus or had gone home by now, even the teachers, so it was strange to see someone still waiting.

I rode up the hill, pumping hard, and was out of breath when I reached the top. Matt Vega shrank back toward the brick wall like I was some kind of monster.

"What are you doing here?" I said.

"Waiting on my dad."

"Why don't you ride the bus?"

"Bus doesn't go to our house."

I tried to choose my next words carefully, but I guess there's no good way to ask somebody exactly where they live.

He backed away a little farther and looked at his backpack. "Ernie told me you were asking about me."

"Yeah, I was just . . . you know, trying to find out more. . . ." I stuttered and sputtered.

Matt looked down at his arm.

"That's a nasty-looking bruise," I said. "What happened?"

He pulled his sleeve down quickly. "Nothing."

"Is that part of your disease?" I said without thinking.

Matt stared like I had seven heads. "What are you talking about?"

A car zoomed up to the parking lot. Mud was caked on the side and under the car, like it had been a year since it had been cleaned.

"Guess this is your dad. Where do you guys live?"

Matt gritted his teeth. "Stop trying to find out stuff. You're just going to get in trouble."

The man in the car rolled the passenger window down and leaned over. No mustache or beard, no ponytail, no tattoos (as far as I could tell). Just a crooked smile and sunglasses sliding down his nose. "Help you with something?" he snarled.

I stared back.

Matt got in and closed the door.

"Who's this punk?" his dad said.

"Nobody."

The man threw the car into gear, and dirt and gravel flew past and slammed the wall behind me. Matt stared out the back window, tight-lipped and looking scared.

Was he scared of me or for me?

CHAPTER 51

❀ Ashley ❀

I looked up all the towns in Texas that started with an *L* and found it overwhelming. Lampasas, Laredo, Liberty, Longview, Lubbock, and about 100 more.

I did another search for oil refineries and oil drilling in Texas, which narrowed the search a little. Trying to figure out a person's past seems fun and exciting, but it can also be really boring and produce a lot of dead ends. The hardest part about any detective work is patience—and it can be your biggest weapon.

I racked my brain, trying to think of anyone who would know where Boo might have lived. Then I remembered Boo's toady little friend who had tried to take our ATVs in the spring, way before school was out. That kid was in ninth grade now, probably bossing other kids or getting beat up. I grabbed our yearbook from the year before and flipped to the eighth-grade section.

I spotted the kid between two pretty girls. His name was Jared Snodgrass, and I instantly felt sorry for him. How he had linked with Boo Heckler, I had no idea, but maybe he just didn't like his name—it made me think of sneezing on a lawn—and wanted to get back at the world.

I found four local listings for *Snodgrass,* eliminating two because they were in another school district. I dialed the other two and scored on the second one.

A young girl answered, and I asked if I could speak with Jared. She giggled and cooed, "Some girl for you!"

I immediately recognized his voice—nasal, like his nose was plugged, and high-pitched, like the whine of a teakettle about to explode.

"Hi, I'm a classmate of Aaron Heckler's."

"Yeah?"

"Somebody said he used to live in Texas. Do you—?"

"Why don't you ask him?"

"Well, he's kind of ticked off at me right now."

Jared chuckled. "Aaron's got a girlfriend? That's funny. What's your name?"

"Well, that's not important—"

"It is if you want my help."

"Ashley."

"Ashley," he said. He laughed more. "Yeah, Texas."

"Do you know what town?"

"Texas is all the same to me. Hot and flat."

I was about to hang up when he said, "But I remember the name of the company his dad used to work for." He told me the name. "So you're really going out with Aaron?"

I hesitated. "You could say I'm weighing all my options."

"What?"

"Thanks, Jared," I said, hanging up.

CHAPTER 52

☺ *Bryce* ☺

Ashley was on the phone when I got home, so I left a note for Mom saying I might be late to dinner. After filling the tank on my ATV, I took off toward the alpaca farm.

It hadn't hit me until Matt's dad pulled away that some of the dirt on his hot rod wasn't red. The dirt roads around our place are all clay, but one trail past the alpaca farm was gray.

I zoomed past the farm, kicking up dust. When I saw a car coming the other way, I got off the road and drove through some pasture. I had to wipe the dust from my visor a couple of times, but I finally made it to what looked like a trail between two huge boulders. This was certainly no driveway, and there was no mailbox within half a mile.

I drove up the trail, which was in shade from the rocks all day so it was muddy. Trees at the top blocked the view. I followed the trail straight down, spinning and sliding in the loose rock and dirt. Another 100 yards and I came to a dry road that wound the other way. This most definitely was a driveway.

I sat on my ATV, heart pounding, wondering what to do, when a streak of light flashed in the distance. A car churned along the driveway, the sun glinting off its windshield.

I turned around as fast as I could and raced for the trees. If it was Matt's dad, I figured he'd chew me out for being on his property. Or worse.

I made it to the trees and turned around. To my relief, the car didn't turn onto the trail but kept going. I figured the road through the rocks was a shortcut they used, but why? After the car passed, I waited a few minutes, then rode through the tall grass and followed the driveway through the pasture. I'd never been back this way, so I made sure I went slow, testing for culverts or hidden drop-offs.

I couldn't see Pikes Peak or the Front Range from here, but it was still a pretty view.

I came over a small ridge and saw that the driveway wound like a white snake through pasture, with no house in sight. Something about the place gave me the willies, like I shouldn't go any farther, but another part of me knew that if I didn't go for it now, I never would.

I turned off the engine. Somewhere in the distance another engine came to life, and I decided to get out of there. Fast.

I flew across the meadow toward a line of trees, hoping no one would spot me. The ground dipped, then slanted unexpectedly. The front-right tire hit a rut, and the left careened off a rock. I hit the brakes, but it was too late.

The ATV flipped and I went down.

CHAPTER 53

✖ Ashley ✖

The company Jared had told me about had three locations in Texas: Houston, Odessa, and Lufkin. Bingo. I got on the Internet and located Lufkin in the middle-eastern part of the state, not far from the Louisiana border.

Then I looked up newspapers near Lufkin. Unfortunately, they were small and didn't file their stories online. I searched for Houston and found the *Chronicle,* a huge paper with online resources.

A bunch of Lufkin stories came up. I typed in *Heckler* and got several stories about politicians being shouted at during a speech. I set the time to search to five years instead of one, and several other stories popped up. None mentioned anything about Boo or his family.

I typed in *Heckler accident,* and a message said, *Your search produced no matches.* I typed in *Heckler fire, Heckler drowning,* and anything else bad that could have happened. Not until I typed in *Heckler death* did a headline appear.

"Death Raises Questions" had a dollar sign next to it, signaling that if I wanted to read it I would have to pay. I'd need a credit card.

The phone rang.

It was Bryce, and he had a bad connection. "I need your help."

"Why? Where are you?"

"Get a chain from the barn and bring your ATV past the alpaca farm."

"How far?"

"Hurry!"

I bookmarked the Web site and ran to the barn.

CHAPTER 54

◯ *Bryce* ◯

I had jumped off before the ATV could fall on me. I lay in the tall grass until the car passed. When I was sure it was gone I ran for the ridge and dialed Ashley.

The phone showed almost no bars, and I was relieved when she picked up. I scampered up the ridge to a bunch of rocks that sat among the trees like they'd been thrown there thousands of years ago. I crawled atop one and looked out over the valley. I followed the white driveway that snaked into the trees and saw the top of a house in the distance. At least there was a house there.

About a half hour went by before I heard the Ashleymobile. I ran near the road, waving, and showed Ashley the way over the hill. She gave me a weird look, then hit the trail.

I met her on the other side and explained what had happened and my plan.

She looked at the sky, and I could tell she was judging how much light we had. "Mom's bringing dinner home," she said.

I kicked at the dirt. Mom's dinners are okay, but when she brings stuff home it's really good. "We'll just call her and explain I got stuck."

I rode on the back of Ashley's ATV as she carefully made her way through the tall grass. I wished I'd driven that way. When we reached my ATV she gave a low whistle. "You're lucky. It would have taken an ambulance a year to get here."

I pointed to the house. "What do you think they're doing way out here? I didn't even know there was a house in these woods."

I hooked the chain to the back of Ashley's ATV and the other end to the metal bar on the back of mine. I pushed as she inched forward, and we finally got the thing turned upright. I couldn't get it started. The engine didn't even sputter.

"Let it sit awhile," I said. "Line's probably flooded. Let's take a look at the house. Maybe Matt lives there."

"We're in enough trouble. We can come back for your—"

"Fine. I'll go myself." I headed for the driveway.

"Oh, all right," she said. "But if we hear anybody, we're heading home on my ATV, got it?"

CHAPTER 55

❀ Ashley ❀

Bryce and I crept through the grass, staying low and hiding behind the occasional pine. Everything in me said we should avoid this place and people who seem to be hiding. But I was also excited. We were actually doing something dangerous for a change.

"There's the house," Bryce whispered as we crouched behind scrub oak.

I expected an old log cabin or a ramshackle lean-to. Instead, it was a brick ranch with no garage but a little shed behind it. Someone had tried to landscape the yard, but now huge weeds grew near the walk and the rock wall was crumbling.

Beside the shed sat a mountain of stuffed trash bags. I wondered if it was the same kind of smelly stuff we had seen thrown out a few days before.

Curtains covered the windows, and the house looked deserted. Bryce moved toward the back, but I grabbed his shirt. "Let's go back and see if your ATV will start."

"I want to check out that shed."

He moved like a long-tailed cat in a room full of rocking chairs. I followed closely.

There was a funny odor at the windowless shed, and I couldn't remember where I'd smelled it before. The door was locked. Bryce tried to peer through the slats, but it was dark inside.

Dust rose behind us, and my heart pounded as tires on dirt and gravel drummed over the meadow.

"No way we can make it back to our ATVs without them seeing us," I said.

The car careened around a curve—it was nearly to the house.

CHAPTER 56

☺ *Bryce* ☺

Some decisions you regret. Like the time I was playing third base with one out, runners on second and third, and the batter bunted. My first thought was to rush in, grab the ball with my bare hand, and throw the guy out. We were up by a run, and all we needed were two more outs.

The problem was that I didn't get a good grip on the ball, and the thing went flying about 20 feet over the head of our first baseman. Yao Ming couldn't have caught it. Two runs scored and we lost. The kid who had scored from second danced like a cheerleader in front of their dugout while I knelt in the dirt a few feet from home plate.

I felt the same way now as we sat with our backs to the hot brick wall of the house. Ashley asked why I chose to drag her here instead of behind the shed or out in the field. I acted like I knew exactly why, but I wasn't even able to convince myself.

The car roared up, and dust rolled over the house. No wonder all the windows had dust on them. The windows on this side of the house had black plastic bags taped to the inside. Strange, especially out here in the wilderness.

Ashley scowled. "Did you hear that?"

Voices on the other side of the house had drowned out whatever it was—a man and a woman arguing. The man couldn't finish one sentence without cursing at least twice.

"Matt, get in here!" the woman yelled.

Ashley looked at me with wide eyes.

CHAPTER 57

❋ Ashley ❋

Another car zoomed up. More yelling. Car doors slamming. People laughing. Someone yelped, and I figured it was Matt. This place gave me the creeps.

God, help us get out of here, I prayed.

The man hollered and something crashed inside. The front door opened and closed again. Footsteps approached the side of the house. I pressed back as close to the bricks as I could and held my breath.

When the shed lock clicked, I saw a young kid the color of Elmer's glue. His shoulders were slumped, and he moved like a

boxer who had just been knocked down and was making his way
back to his corner.

"That's Matt," Bryce mouthed.

Matt hung the lock on the metal fastener and opened the door.
He glanced back and saw us, and I thought his mouth would fall to
the ground. He moved inside, quickly grabbed two white bottles,
closed and locked the door, then walked toward us.

"What are you doing here?" he whispered. "You want to get
hurt? Get out before they see you. When you hear the front door
open, take off through the field."

Bryce nodded. "What's going on?"

"Just go, okay?"

"Matt?!" a woman yelled.

He stiffened and scurried past the side of the house.

When the door opened and closed, Bryce and I took off for the
weeds. Someone screamed, which made me move faster, but I
didn't look back. I sprinted into the tall grass and dived headfirst.
Bryce landed beside me with a thud.

"Stupid!" someone shouted. "What were you thinking?"

A slap.

"I didn't mean to drop it," Matt said, crying.

"We have to help him," Bryce said.

"Not now," I said. "Let's go home."

Bryce nodded. We rose and were about to run when his cell
phone rang. Loud.

CHAPTER 58

☺ *Bryce* ☺

I turned my phone off before the second ring, then held my breath as the front door opened. The only thing I saw after that was grass, because Ashley and I ducked lower than an ant's navel.

"Somebody leave their phone in the car?" a man hollered.

Another joined him—or maybe spoke through the door. "You must be hearing things."

"No, I heard it. I swear."

A ladybug crawled up a blade of grass in front of me. I wondered if it was really a female. What would you call a male ladybug? Funny what you focus on when your life is about to end.

Footsteps crunched through the gravel, then *swish, swish,* *swish*ed into the grass. What would they do if they found us?

Through the grass I saw a man scratch his head, look at the shed, and check behind the house. Finally, he turned and walked inside.

Ashley started to move as soon as the door closed, but I grabbed her arm. A few seconds after the guy went inside, curtains parted at a window.

"Stay still until we know they're not looking," I said.

Ashley put her head on the ground and her shoulders shook. I put a hand on her back, thinking she was crying. But she was laughing.

"I was just thinking how funny it would be if these people were missionaries or something."

"Swearing missionaries?" I said. "These people are only missionaries for Glad trash bags."

She stopped laughing. "It was really weird. When I was near the vent, I guess from the laundry room, I swear I heard somebody singing."

The light faded as the sun dipped below the horizon. The days were getting shorter as we made that slow climb toward winter.

"Who called?" Ashley said.

"Didn't see, but I bet it was Mom."

"She'll be ticked about dinner."

"I'd rather survive this."

When we detected no movement inside we finally raced back to the ATVs.

CHAPTER 59

✖ Ashley ✖

It was the longest run of my life—even harder than the mile Coach Baldwin made us run last year. I kept thinking someone would chase us in their car, but we made it without a problem— other than not being able to breathe.

I let Bryce try his ATV first, in case he couldn't get it started and needed to ride with me. He slammed his helmet on and turned the key. The engine sparked to life.

I noticed someone moving at the front of the house, pointing at us.

"Come on!" Bryce said in my headset.

We zipped through the fields and up the side of the hill to the shortcut. When we got to the top, I saw a Jeep barreling out of the driveway toward us.

We rode over the rocky ledge, Bryce taking the road a lot faster than me. He's an animal when it comes to speed. He loves it.

When we were back on the main road, Bryce suggested we get to the Morris farm as fast as we could through the back gate. We cut through a pasture and into more trees, dodging them as we rocketed toward the farm. We didn't see the Jeep until we were almost to the gate. It zigzagged down the road, trying to find us. We stopped in the trees and watched the Jeep pass while Buck, the Morrises' dog, ran back and forth along the fence.

Bryce called Mom. "Sorry we're late, but Ashley and I ran into something out here. We'll be home before dark."

CHAPTER 60

☺ *Bryce* ☺

We got the cold stare from Mom as we ate. I could tell she was trying to figure out what we'd been up to, but Ashley and I kept our heads down and told her how good everything was.

Randy, Leigh's boyfriend, lightened things by telling us about football practice and how hot it had been the past few days. A lot of guys tossed their Gatorade, and Randy said it was colorful with all the shades of green and red and blue. Ashley didn't seem interested in the rest of her dinner, but it didn't bother me.

Later Ashley and I met in my room, where we brainstormed and wrote as many ideas as we could.

"The house could be an FBI hideout for some secret operation," Ashley said.

"Why would they be treating a kid like Matt so badly?"

She shrugged. "The black plastic bags could be to keep the light out of a room—you know, so they could develop pictures. Developing chemicals could be what was in the white bottles."

"Why wouldn't they go digital?"

We wrote down stuff like *drug smuggling* and *counterfeiting,* but we never felt any closer to the truth than we had been at the beginning.

"Maybe these people aren't doing anything illegal," I said. "Maybe they just want to be left alone."

"What if they've escaped from prison?"

"Why would they have Matt with them? And why would they let him go to school?" I paused. "And who was that you heard singing?"

"It sounded like a kid."

"Couldn't have been Matt," I said. "He wasn't home yet."

Ashley nodded, then opened the door and peeked downstairs. "I want to get on the computer, but everybody's in the living room."

"What are you looking up?"

She told me what she'd found out about Boo, and I teased her about getting info about her future husband.

She just stared at me with those big eyes. "I'm serious, Bryce. Mrs. Ogilvie says there's always some reason people act the way they do. If they're mean, they've probably had something bad happen to them."

Mrs. Ogilvie is the counselor at church who Ashley and I go to every other week. "Nothing about Boo Heckler makes sense," I said.

Someone knocked at the door—softly.

Ashley shrugged.

"Come in," I said.

CHAPTER 61

✖ Ashley ✖

Randy looked over his shoulder and quietly closed the door. "Hey."

"Hey," Bryce and I said.

He crossed his arms, then uncrossed them and put his hands in his pockets, then leaned against the wall and scratched his head.

"Something wrong?" I said. I knew he didn't have fleas.

"No," he said too quickly. "I just wanted your opinion about something."

"About Leigh?" I said.

He nodded and looked at Bryce's baseball collection.

Bryce said, "You gonna ask her to marry you?"

Randy's head snapped at him faster than a wide receiver in traffic. "No, nothing like that. It's just that . . . well, I was wondering, since you guys . . . I mean, you know that Leigh . . ." His face turned red, and he shifted against the wall for the 50th time. It was really kind of cute.

He took a deep breath. "See, I've been going to your church and stuff is starting to—I don't know, sort of make sense, I guess."

"That's great," Bryce said.

"Yeah, but the more I find out at church, the bigger differences I see between Leigh and me. I know how she feels about all that stuff. The whole thing turns her off. I don't even talk about it with her."

"So you've decided to become a Christian?" I said.

He dipped his head. "Well, let's say I'm still deciding. I'm not sure about some things. . . ."

"We've been working on Leigh for a long time," Bryce said. "Most of the time she just rolls her eyes."

"She's been so hurt," I said, and I thought about Boo. "Sometimes people can't forgive God, even though they say they don't believe in him."

"Forgive him for her mom and sister?" Randy said.

I nodded.

"You know, Randy," Bryce said, "what Leigh does about God is between her and him. But it sounds like God is working on you. Maybe you taking the next step will force Leigh to do something too. Maybe it won't. But you have to do what you have to do."

Randy nodded, but he looked troubled. "It's just that I don't think she'd stay with me if I became some kind of religious wacko."

"That's what you're afraid of?"

"I know better, but I don't want to wind up wearing Jesus stickers on my jersey and carrying a Bible to class and preaching to people."

I covered my mouth to keep from laughing at the thought of Randy as a Football Preacher.

"You don't have to do any of that," Bryce said. "God will show you—"

The door opened and Leigh stepped inside.

Randy rubbed his neck. "Just catching up with your brother and sister."

CHAPTER 62

☻ *Bryce* ☻

Mr. Gminski came in before first period the next morn-ing and asked how I was doing. Usually I just say fine, but for some reason I felt like actually telling him. I said something was bothering me about one of the sixth graders, "and I'm not sure what to do."

"What's the nature of the difficulty?"

Mr. Gminski talks like that. He uses big words, not because he's trying to impress us or anything, but because, well, he knows what they mean. He's a square-looking man, with wide shoulders and about 30 pounds too much around his middle.

I didn't tell him Matt's name, but I told him in a vague way what Ashley and I had seen.

"I appreciate that you care about this young man," Mr. Gminski said. "You shouldn't jump to conclusions, but he might need help."

"What if he doesn't want help?"

Mr. Gminski frowned. "Sometimes the one who asks you to leave him alone needs the most help."

CHAPTER 63

✖ Ashley ✖

Boo wandered into Spanish and flipped a couple of people in the head as he walked by.

"Hi, Fernando," I said cheerily.

He looked away.

I got Hayley's attention. "Got a question. I'm researching a town in Texas. You have relatives down there, don't you?"

"Lots," Hayley said. "What town?"

"Lufkin," I said, watching Boo out of the corner of my eye.

He flinched and glanced at me.

"My relatives live near Dallas," Hayley said. "What are you trying to find out?"

"Just stuff about the area. I'm looking at old news reports."

Boo stared at me. I could tell I'd hit a nerve.

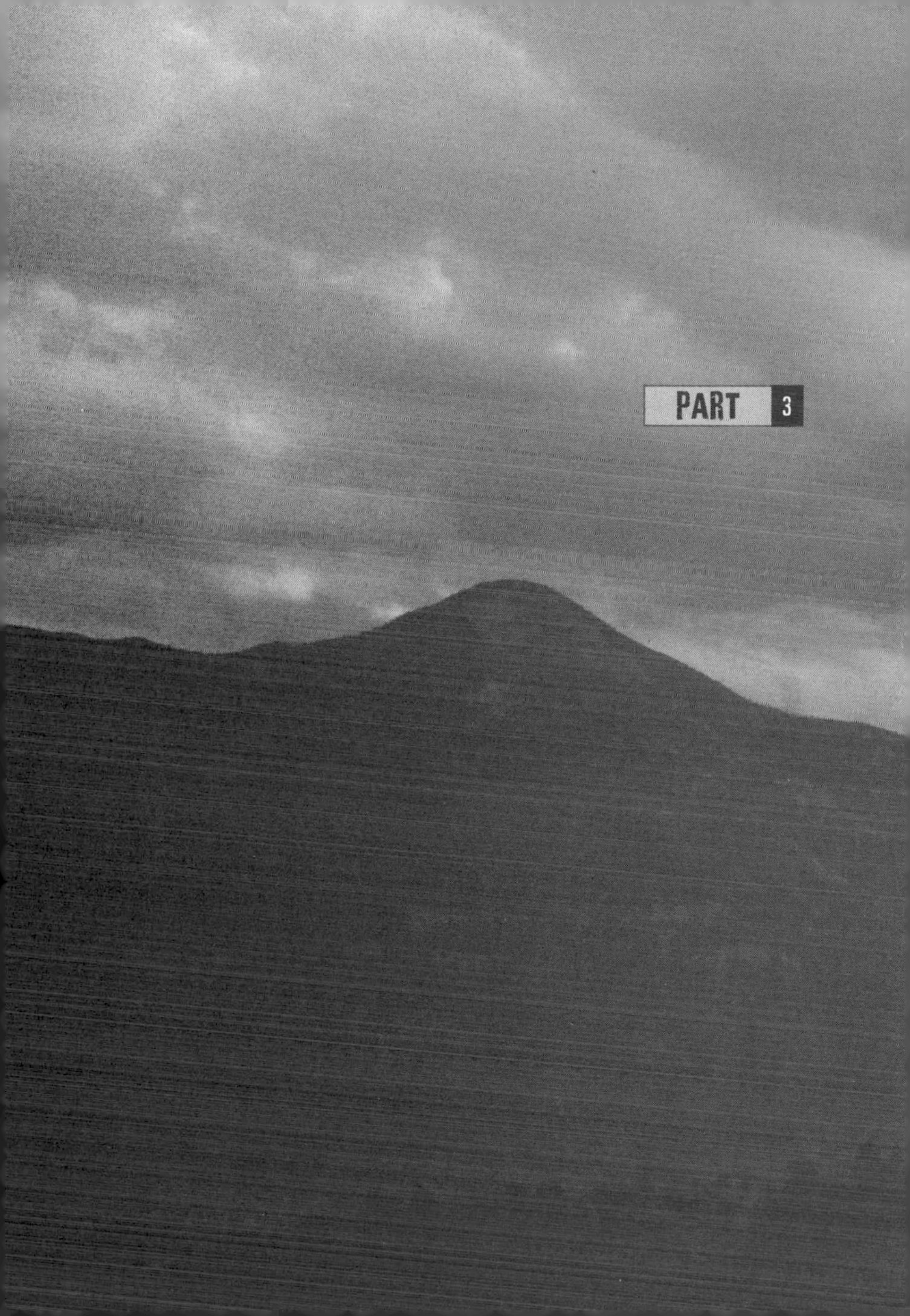

PART 3

CHAPTER 64

She kept quiet, hoping that if she tried something other than crying for food and water they might bring it sooner. They didn't. Maybe they thought she was sleeping.

She listened closely. When they were in the next room, she could hear them talking, making noises, watching television, or listening to the radio.

Over the last few days she had used the end of a coat hanger to slowly dig a tiny hole in the wall, just enough to see through. Light peeked in, and she thought it was the most wonderful thing. She could see a mirror above the old dresser, and through it, a little of the sky. Every now and then a bird flew over, or she heard a helicopter or an airplane.

The radio was her favorite. She loved the music. Even people talking about politics and elections kept her company.

Someone was in the next room. She heard coat hangers clink. Someone else walked in.

"It's just a couple of kids, that's all," her father said. "We can take care of them."

"All we need is kids snooping around. Remember last time? I don't want another scene like that."

"It's not going to happen again," her father said. "We stay a few more days, sell the rest, and head north. Maybe Montana or Wyoming. I've got people up there who say they know the perfect place."

"You said we'd stay a year. That's why we let Matt start school."

"He'll keep going until we leave. We don't want anyone asking questions."

"I've got some teacher's meeting this afternoon," her mother said.

"Tell them you're sick. Nosy teachers are the last things we need."

There was a long silence. Finally her mother spoke. "What about . . . ?"

She knew they were talking about her. She wondered if they ever spoke her name. Why did they hate her? Because she talked to people in the last town? The woman next door seemed to like her and gave her food. But in the middle of the night they had moved, just picked up and left.

"We can't trust her," her father said. "The town's too close. Next stop, we'll find a place miles from everything else and we won't have to worry."

A tear leaked as she strained to see her mother and father. But she couldn't see them.

CHAPTER 65

☻ *Bryce* ☻

It was important to explain to Matt why Ashley and I had
been at his house, but I couldn't find him.

I went to the office at lunch and asked the secretary if Matt was
called in absent. She scanned the list and shook her head.

"Mr. Timberline." It was our principal, Mr. Bookman. He said it
as if he was happy he'd recognized a student, not as if he liked me.
"You attend the church that sponsored the protest last week, right?"

"It wasn't a protest, sir," I said. "And those were kids from a lot of
different churches, not just ours."

"I see. Well, I talked with someone named Andy. Do you know him?"

No wonder he wanted to talk to me. He was scared. "Sure, he's our youth pastor."

Out of the corner of my eye I saw Matt walking into the boys' bathroom.

Mr. Bookman stepped closer. "He told me there isn't going to be a lawsuit, that your sister said something at a meeting that helped change people's minds."

"That's great," I said. "Would you excuse me, please?"

"Certainly."

I raced toward the bathroom and banged in. I bent and saw Matt's ratty shoes in one of the stalls. I hung my backpack on a hook and washed my hands, taking my time.

Finally, Matt shuffled to a sink, his eyes on the floor.

"Matt," I said, trying not to startle him. It didn't work. He looked at me like I had horns and a pitchfork. "Can I talk with you a minute?"

"What were you doing at my house?" His eyes were fiery and his teeth clenched. "Are you crazy?"

"Had some trouble with my ATV. Called my sister, but before we could get it started, we thought we'd stop by. What's going on?"

Matt scrubbed his hands like he was going into surgery. "I told you to stay away from me, okay?"

"Look, I have no idea what's going on, but if you need help—"

He slammed the paper-towel dispenser with his fist, and it jammed. He hit it a couple more times, then wiped his hands on his pants. "You have no idea how much trouble you could cause. Do you know what they're making back there?"

"No, but that's why—"

"Don't ever come near our place, understand?"

"I'm just trying to help."

"You can't help. You're only going to make it worse for me and . . . for all of us. Promise you won't talk to me or come near my house again."

"Matt, whatever's going on, I can help. God can help."

He shook his head. "God forgot about us a long time ago."

CHAPTER 66

❇ Ashley ❇

I raced home before Bryce. I had to find out more about Boo and what had happened in Lufkin. I was so winded that I let my bike fall in the grass and stumbled up the front steps.

Leigh's purse and books lay on the entry table. *Please don't let her be on the computer,* I prayed.

Leigh stared at the computer screen, eating from a yogurt container. She didn't even look up.

I grabbed a glass of ice water and gulped it as I watched her. She carefully swiped the spoon around the yogurt, getting every last molecule. I knew if I asked to use the computer, she'd take another 20 minutes.

"Know where Mom is?" I said.

"Took Dylan to the store. She said to remind you to clean the litter box."

Great. Something to kill time.

Patches stays in my room, except when she goes to the litter box or eats in a little storage room at the end of our hall. She's a calico, which means she has all kinds of colors. She has the greenest eyes you've ever seen. Mom doesn't like all the hair she sheds, but I love curling up with her and listening to her purr.

I took one of the big trash bags from under the kitchen sink and trudged upstairs. Patches lay on my bed, her tail twitching, eyes blinking, lost in some daydream. What does a cat do on its day off? Can't lie around. That's its job.

I was putting the new liner in the litter box when something clicked in my brain. This was the same smell I'd noticed at Matt's house. Bizarre.

I sat in the hall, thinking. Could Matt's parents be running an illegal cat farm? What is an illegal cat farm? One that kills cats and sells the meat to bad restaurants? (We'd heard back when we lived in Chicago that one restaurant near a veterinarian stole sick cats and used the meat. It wasn't true, of course, but it grossed out a lot of people. The restaurant finally closed.) Now I had something else to look up on the Internet.

When I got back to the kitchen, Leigh stood and grabbed the phone. "You can use the computer now."

I plopped into the chair before she changed her mind and soon found the *Houston Chronicle*. I had forgotten that it cost money to read the story. As soon as Leigh got off the phone I called Mom and got permission to use her card number, promising, of course, to pay her back.

CHAPTER 67

☻ *Bryce* ☻

Ashley was on the phone with Mom when I got home. I waited around to ask if she wanted to go check out Matt's place from a high bluff, but she seemed engrossed in the computer. I grabbed a couple packages of fruit snacks, took our telescope apart, and used a strap to sling the main part over my back.

I had a plan. I drove past the Morrises' barn but didn't want anyone hearing the engine, so I stopped and walked the rest of the way to the bluff overlooking Matt's house. Boulders were scattered around a little trail that looked like it had been made by deer.

This place reminded me of Little Round Top at Gettysburg, with pine trees all around and rocks to climb. I found a spot where I could steady the telescope and pointed it toward Matt's house.

Several cars were parked in front, and the door to the shed was open, which made me think they might be making more of whatever scared Matt.

If people were doing something bad, you'd think he'd tell his parents. Unless his parents . . . I remembered the bruises on his arms and him crying at his house. Were they hurting him? I've heard that even kids who are abused sometimes tend to protect their parents.

Something moved in the field beside the house, and I focused on three deer, their heads to the ground. Suddenly they raised and looked in my direction, then bolted toward the tree line.

Something moved behind me, and the hair on the back of my neck stood straight up.

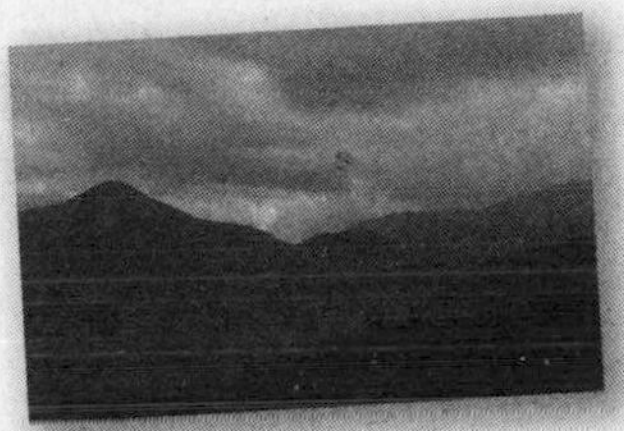

CHAPTER 68

Ashley

I read the article breathlessly. It had cost me about five cents a word, so I drank in every detail.

> Death Raises Questions
>
> LUFKIN—The death of a four-year-old girl here has raised more questions about illegal aliens, their rights, and parental responsibility.
>
> A week ago, Cesar Rodriguez, an illegal alien, borrowed a car and went for a drive—the first of his life. He had no driver's license, little experience behind the wheel—family

members say he'd mostly driven tractors—and didn't understand enough English to read street signs. Onlookers say he was driving as if drunk, though tests proved negative for alcohol.

Police say Rodriguez careened through a parking lot, raced across a basketball court, and smashed into a swing set, killing four-year-old Shelly Heckler. Rodriguez fled the scene.

The girl's parents, Mr. and Mrs. Darryl Heckler, heard of their daughter's death from a radio report and said they'd had no idea she was at the park. The family home is half a mile away.

The rest of the article posed questions about what should be done with illegal aliens and whether the parents were responsible for letting a four-year-old wander.

Maybe this was why Boo was so mean to Cindy Lopez. Maybe he hated Spanish class and Spanish people and Mrs. Sanchez because of what had happened to his sister. Could it be that he was supposed to have been watching her?

☾ *Bryce* ☾

If an animal was behind me, I'd look like a human Happy Meal. If it was a human . . . well, I didn't want to think about that.

I tried to swallow and breathe, but my heart was beating so fast and my stomach had turned so many times that I thought I was going to toss my fruit snacks.

"Whatcha lookin' at?" someone said.

I almost jumped out of my skin. I whirled to see Kyle, the Morrises' oldest son.

He laughed when he saw the look on my face.

"You shouldn't sneak up behind people like that," I said, a hand over my heart. It had slowed to about a million beats per minute.

He looked at my telescope, then at the house in the clearing. "I thought those people moved out."

"Do you know who owns that land?"

"Yeah, Mr. Carswell. He said Dad could take us hunting, and there's a fish pond over there."

"Do you know who those people are?"

Kyle shook his head.

"Does Mr. Carswell live in town?"

He nodded. "Can I look through your telescope?"

I showed him how, and while he was looking I called information and asked for the number of a Carswell in Red Rock. Fortunately there was only one.

I reached Mr. Carswell and introduced myself, telling him that my sister and I had an alpaca at the Morris farm.

"I know them well," he said. "Good people."

"Well, I'm up behind their property, looking at the house down in the clearing. Kyle Morris said it was yours."

Mr. Carswell paused, and I could only imagine him wondering what in the world I was driving at. "Yes," he said. "That's my property. Why?"

"I was just wondering about the people renting from you. One of their kids goes to school with me, and I'm kind of worried about him."

"Kids? I don't know anything about children living there. I rented to a couple who said they wanted to get back to nature."

"Hey, Bryce?" Kyle said.

"Thanks so much, sir. Sorry to bother you. Good-bye."

"Those people down there in front of the house," Kyle said, still looking through the telescope. "Why are they all so skinny?"

I knelt and looked through the scope. Kyle was right. They were all thin, and a couple of people scratched their necks and faces. One guy near a car had something up to his face.

Binoculars. And he was looking straight at me. When he pointed, I grabbed my telescope and Kyle and ran down the hill.

CHAPTER 70

❈ Ashley ❈

It was a long ride to Boo Heckler's house, mostly uphill, but I just had to go. Their gravel road pitched down, and I rode slowly, taking in the tall pines and scattered boulders. A crude tree house sat between two trees, with slats nailed into one for a ladder. It looked like kid heaven, where you could explore and pretend you were a pirate or a space alien or just about anything.

I watched for any sign of Boo, ready to escape if he came out, but the house looked quiet. I stopped and stared, thinking that this was a stupid idea and there was no way I was going to accomplish anything, when a girl walked out, brushed a wisp of hair from her face, and headed for the mailbox. She was pretty, if you could get past her clumpy hair and dirty fingernails. A day at a salon would make her one of those kids you see in the Kohl's ads, but I figured that probably wasn't going to happen.

I rode over as she opened the box and looked inside. "Hi, I'm Ashley."

"Hi," she said, looking back warily.

"I go to school with Aaron."

"Oh. I'm Jessie."

"I haven't seen you at the middle school."

"I'm in fifth grade."

"Oh, so next year. You'll like it. Hey, you guys used to live in Lufkin, didn't you?"

She smiled and nodded. "How'd you know that?"

I shrugged.

She pulled the mail from the box, and her face fell when she scanned the envelopes.

"I hate waiting for stuff to come in the mail," I said.

She looked up. "A book from Amazon was supposed to be here by now."

I wanted to keep her there, but she closed the mailbox and turned toward the house.

"Can I ask you something?" I said. "About Shelly."

Jessie stiffened and turned. "You know about her?"

"Only a little."

She bit her lip and glanced at the house. Then her eyes lit up. "Meet me at the tree house in five minutes."

CHAPTER 71

☺ *Bryce* ☺

I pulled Kyle down the hill to my ATV, and I let him wear the helmet. I had to make it to the Morris farm fast.

I parked behind their house and followed Kyle inside. Mrs. Morris was in the kitchen, and Kyle's two little brothers sounded like they were fighting downstairs. Kyle told his mom about the skinny people at the house in the clearing.

"Oh, really?" she said, concentrating on some recipe.

Kyle went downstairs, so I asked Mrs. Morris if I could use their computer to check something on the Internet and she said sure. I pulled up a search engine, one on which you can type questions and get answers. I typed *skinny, scratch faces, coffee filters, chemicals?*

The answer pointed me to several Web sites on how to lose weight, how to make espresso at home, and even a scuba Web site. I needed to refine my question.

I tried again, but got another page of Web sites about how French fries make people skinny. I came up empty on the next few searches, then remembered some of the things I'd seen in the trash bags. I typed in *antifreeze, duct tape, coffee filters* and then added the name of the medicine Matt and his mom had bought.

Suddenly I was directed to a news article about a small town in Kansas, and I could tell from the first paragraph that I was on to something. It talked about the same smell I'd noticed around the house and gave the reason why people lost weight and scratched at their faces and created sores.

When I'd read the whole thing, I was more scared than ever about Matt and his family.

CHAPTER 72

❀ Ashley ❀

The tree house didn't have much in it. Just a wood floor and some things nailed to the wall. An empty water bottle and a couple of Safeway bags lay in the corner.

I was afraid Jessie wouldn't come out and I'd be waiting here until dark. Or worse, that she'd tell Boo and he'd come throw rocks at me. But a few minutes after I'd climbed the tree, Jessie came bounding out of the house.

"How old were you when this happened?" I said.

"I was in first grade. Shelly was two years younger than me. She'd be nine now. We used to play with horses and dolls and stuff.

She had these cute, stubby little teeth, and when she laughed . . ."
Jessie grabbed one of the Safeway bags and pulled out an old wallet.
Inside was a picture of Jessie, her hair short and her arms tanned,
smiling, one arm around a smaller girl with blonde hair. "This was a
couple of weeks before it happened."

"How did your brother get along with her?"

"Aaron loved her. Used to pick her up and throw her over his
shoulder. He was strong even back then. Sometimes Mom and Dad
would have him babysit."

I couldn't imagine Boo babysitting anyone. "So he wasn't . . . ?"
I stopped, not wanting to offend her.

"As mean as he is now?" she said.

I nodded.

"Aaron thinks the whole thing was his fault. He took her to the
park without Mom and Dad knowing. Then a friend of his came
along, and they went across the street to this ice-cream shop. Aaron
said he watched her swinging the whole time, that he didn't take his
eyes off her. But when that guy in the car crashed into the play-
ground . . ."

She put her hands to her face and wiped her eyes. "We don't talk
about it. My mom and dad don't even mention her name."

"Does Aaron?" I said.

She shook her head. "After that he started getting in trouble.
Then we moved away, I guess because of all the memories."

"Did your parents blame him for what happened?"

She shrugged.

Knowing what had happened didn't excuse Boo's behavior or
make it hurt less when he bullied, but it did make me feel sad for him.

CHAPTER 73

☺ *Bryce* ☺

I covered for Ashley at dinner, even though I didn't know where she was. Later, when Sam and I were shooting baskets outside, I said, "You think Ashley and I can camp out over at the Morris farm Thursday? We have Friday off from school."

His shot clunked off the rim, giving me an easy basket. I banked it in and turned to him. "Supposed to be warm."

I could tell he was kicking himself for missing the shot. "Yeah, if it's okay with your mother," he muttered.

"Why do you always say that?" I said, swishing my next shot.

Sam tossed the ball to me. "What do you want me to say?"

"Just say yes. Mom does it. It's like you have to ask her permission all the time. We're your kids too."

Sam eyed me from under the basket. "There some reason why you want to be out *there*? Why not just camp in our backyard?"

"That's for little kids. We've got the new tent, and Mr. Morris said we could come over anytime. Buck will keep wild animals away from us."

Sam nodded. "Tell your mother I said it was okay."

CHAPTER 74

✖ Ashley ✖

I didn't want anything to eat when I got home, so I went up to
my room. I lit my scented candle and opened my journal. I wrote:

> I feel so bad about Aaron. He's been such a bully and so mean that I
> couldn't help but hate him. Maybe hate is too strong. I just wouldn't pick him
> as someone I'd want to sit beside in Spanish.
>
> It makes me wonder what Jesus would say to Aaron. I don't think Jesus
> would be mad at him because he would know how much Aaron's hurting. It
> must eat at him all the time. Maybe he can't forgive himself, and that's why
> he gets in trouble.
>
> I want to treat him differently and try as hard as I can to be nice.

The door opened and I closed my journal.

"Something wrong?" Bryce said.

"Why?"

"Mom said you didn't want dinner or even fresh apple pie. You never pass up pie and ice cream, especially when it's all melted on top and—"

I put up a hand. "Okay, yes, something's wrong. I think we've been wrong about Boo."

I told Bryce the whole story, and he sat there quietly for a long time. Finally he sighed and shook his head. "I don't think I ever thought of Boo as a real person. He's just a big nuisance, like a human hangnail."

"No wonder his parents are having problems," I said. "I can't imagine what it would be like to lose a child."

Bryce said, "You know, this doesn't make Boo any less mean. Just because we found out something about his past doesn't change that."

I nodded. "But it should change the way we treat him."

CHAPTER 75

☻ *Bryce* ☻

Ashley and I got our camping stuff together Thursday after school, and we also packed stuff from Sam's office, like his night-vision binoculars and an air horn that could scare away wild animals. Or wild people.

I had scoped out a place on a grassy knoll hidden by some trees up the mountain behind the Morrises'. We anchored the tent to the trees since the ground was so hard. From there we could easily see Matt's house, but no one could see us unless we started a campfire or turned on flashlights.

When we got our sleeping bags unrolled, I pulled out a bag of

Double Stuf Oreos. (Ashley loves them.) She had eaten her fourth before she narrowed her eyes. "You're setting me up."

I tried to act innocent. "Me?"

"Why'd you bring me out here and remember my favorite cookies?"

"Isn't that what a loving brother is for?"

"Funny. Now tell me."

I took a deep breath. "Have you ever heard of meth?"

"You mean math?"

"No. Meth. Methamphetamines. It's a drug. They also call it crank and a bunch of other names."

"I've heard about it on the news. The police shut down a lab or something in a house in the Springs."

I nodded. "Well, I think Matt's parents might be running a lab here."

CHAPTER 76

✿ Ashley ✿

Bryce had done his homework. The smell from the shed (that reminded me of Patches' cat litter) was the same that people said they noticed around the labs. Bryce said meth makers drain fluid through coffee filters, which explained all the weird stuff in the trash bags.

"Why don't we just call the police?" I said, grabbing another Oreo.

He held up the digital camera. "I want to be 100 percent sure before we get them involved. This is going to mess up Matt's life big-time."

"If his mom and dad are selling drugs, his life is already messed up. What'll happen to Matt if you're right?"

"He'd probably be sent to a foster home or some other kind of facility. Happens a lot with drug busts."

"Sad," I said. "Listen, you're not going down there and taking pictures, are you?"

He pulled out a pair of black sweats, a black shirt, and shoe polish. "I'll rub this on my face, and while I'm down there, you'll be here with the phone."

"No way. I'm not letting you have all the fun."

He pulled out another pair of black sweats and a black shirt. "I thought you'd say that."

CHAPTER 77

☺ *Bryce* ☺

Ashley passed on the shoe polish—she said she'd risk her face picking up a little light. I rubbed it all over my face, and Ashley said it was like I had disappeared, except for the whites of my eyes.

Before heading out we lay back on our sleeping bags and stared at the stars. "You know what they're doing, God," I said. "We don't want to do anything dumb, but I can't help feeling that you're using us to help Matt."

Ashley prayed that we'd find an answer to our questions fast and that no one would get hurt. She also prayed for Matt's parents, that if they were doing illegal stuff they'd be sorry and change. I hadn't thought much of them until she said that.

We put on our helmets and turned up the volume on the micro-
phones so we could communicate with each other by whispering,
even if we got separated.

As we made our way silently down the hill, things were starting
to come together in my head. The medicine from the dollar store
was used for meth. One report said people lost lots of weight and
scratched at imaginary sores when they used the drug. One thing
I didn't know was whether these people were tied in with the
illegal-alien truck.

There were even more cars at the house than there had been the
day before. Thin strips of light glowed around the trash bags in the
windows. The wind whipped that familiar strong smell our direction, and I turned my head. I couldn't imagine actually living in a
house that smelled like that.

We crouched behind some firewood. I handed my phone to
Ashley, and she took it. "Go to the shed," I said. "You'll have a
better angle to watch the house and tell me if anyone's coming. I'll
find a window and get photos. Shouldn't take long."

Ashley took a look around. "I don't like it."

"I'll be in and out before you know it. Go."

CHAPTER 78

✖ Ashley ✖

I crept through the grass to the shed, where I had a good view of the house. A screen door led to the kitchen, and a light was on inside. Music blared, pumping, vibrating the windows.

"I see a window partially open," Bryce said. "Tell me if you see anyone." He darted to the side of the house. "Okay, I can see a little bit of light coming from one of the basement windows."

I heard music coming through louder as Bryce got closer. "Is there anyone in there?" I said.

"I hear people laughing," he said. "It's a window well. I have to climb down—"

"No, absolutely not! I'll call Mom and Sam if you do."

He sighed. "Stop. There's a ladder. I'll see if there's anything..."
His voice trailed off.

"What?"

"Somebody's moving near the window. Hang on."

I stared into the darkness, then focused the night-vision binoculars on the side of the house as Bryce turned and climbed into the window well. In Colorado just about every house has a few windows belowground that have U-shaped metal things to hold the dirt back. People put ladders inside in case there's a fire and you have to crawl out.

When Bryce's head disappeared, I whispered, "What do you see?"

He grunted and I figured he was kneeling. "They have curtains, but I can see a little. It looks like Ms. Prine's science room. All kinds of equipment and stuff."

I tried to imagine the room, but I couldn't. Something in the binoculars took my attention away. The back door opened, and two people came toward me.

CHAPTER 79

☺ *Bryce* ☺

I heard the back door and froze. If anyone came my way, they might see me, so I pressed back against the window well, hoping to melt into the darkness.

"Where are they going?" I whispered.

"My way," Ashley said.

"Run!"

"Can't. Be quiet."

It was weird standing in a window well, listening to your sister get caught. Or was she? I snapped a few pictures of the room, zooming in on some of the equipment. Then I heard voices. At first, I thought they were near me, but then I realized they were coming from Ashley's microphone.

The first was a man's voice. ". . . torch the place and destroy the evidence."

"We're still going to have to run," a woman said.

Matt's mom and dad?

"I told you about Montana. That's where we're headed."

"But those kids, the ones Matt told us about . . ."

"They'll get the police snooping before long. We need to move now. Take the cash from tonight and our stash by the trees. That'll give us a good start."

"What about . . . her?" the woman said.

At first I thought they'd seen Ashley. I was ready to jump out, slam on the air horn, and save her.

"After what she's put us through, I say leave her where she is."

"And Matt?"

"Tell him it was an accident."

The woman: "How do we do it?"

"The shed will go fast. That'll get everybody out of the house. Get our stuff and Matt and get to the car. Pull it out of the way and wait for me."

CHAPTER 80

Ashley

I held my breath as the woman ran to the house. As the man fumbled with cans in the shed, I scampered away and watched him through the binoculars. He opened one can, poured the contents on the ground inside the shed, and backed away.

"Bryce, don't go near that shed," I whispered.

"I'm still at the side of the house."

"Did you hear?"

"Yeah, what do you think they meant by 'stash by the trees'?"

"Hang on—the guy's lighting a match."

The man cupped his hand around the match, but it blew out. He knelt with his back to the wind and struck another. It flashed bright against his hands, and he dropped it. He fell back as the line of liquid caught fire. It took a few seconds to reach the shed. Then I heard a *whomp,* and the shed burst into flames that licked at the wood slats.

"Get behind something," Bryce said. "When that thing blows, it'll—"

An explosion like a million firecrackers made my ears ring as a fireball rose from the shed.

"I'm calling the police," I said. "Bryce, can you hear me?"

"Yeah . . ." His voice was weak. "Go ahead."

I dialed the number, but I had no reception.

People ran out of the house, and another smaller explosion rocked the place. Matt ran for a car with his mother not far behind carrying a duffel bag.

"Go! Go! Go!" the dad yelled. "We've got to get out of here!"

People scattered like ants. I had to get to my brother, so I sprinted for the window well, telling him what I saw as I ran. He was still in the well and looked funny with all that shoe polish running down his face. Though we were a long way away from the shed, the heat was intense.

I helped pull him up. "Some blast, huh?" he said. Some windows had been blown out of the house.

Headlights came on, and car tires spun dirt as we ducked behind the house. I wondered if the whole field and forest could go up, not to mention the alpaca farm on the other side of the hill.

I heard the singing again. Someone humming, like a little doll. It was muffled.

"Bryce, there's somebody else there. And that guy's going to set the house on fire."

"Run for that hill and dial 911. If I find a phone inside, I'll dial from there."

As soon as Bryce was inside, I took off through the field.

Please, God, help him get out of there.

I was well into the field when I heard the air horn. Bryce blasted it like a police siren. Flames licked out of the basement windows.

CHAPTER 81

◔ *Bryce* ◔

Someone was downstairs rummaging around. I grabbed an old phone on the wall but got no dial tone. I yanked a curtain cord down and wrapped it around the air horn. It shrieked loud enough to split my eardrums, so I was glad I had my helmet on.

I raced back through the hall as the basement door flew open. Smoke billowed out. Matt's dad went straight for the air horn. I ducked into the bathroom and held my breath. He must have thrown the air horn downstairs, because it banged against something and stopped. Then the front door opened and slammed. I heard yelling in the yard. Something about the place going up.

I heard coughing and moved to the end of the hall. On one side was an empty room except for a bed and dresser. On the other side was a shut door. I tried the knob. It was unlocked, but there was a bolt on the outside.

"Hey! Fire! Come out!"

More coughing and whimpering. Someone crying.

I slid the latch back and pushed the door open. A laundry room. Clothes in dirty piles.

"Anybody in here?" I yelled.

No response.

A fresh wave of smoke met me. The last car in front of the house threw gravel as it sped toward the long driveway.

"Help me," a weak voice said. It sounded like it was coming from the laundry room.

Behind brooms and an ancient vacuum cleaner I found a closet. It, too, had a sliding bolt lock. I slid it open, turned the knob, and opened the door.

CHAPTER 82

✖ Ashley ✖

I finally got cell-phone reception as I climbed the hill. I told the operator where we were, that there was a fire, and that we needed the police.

"My brother is still in the house, and it's burning." That's when it sunk in: maybe I'd never see Bryce again.

"Want me to stay on the line until the police get there?" she said.

My voice caught and I choked, "No, I'm okay." I told her the people who were leaving were dealing drugs and had set the fire.

She said the police would intercept them if they could find the right road and get there in time.

I raced back downhill. The burning shed had started a grass fire, and I had to run around it. As I came up over a little knoll, the house exploded in a blinding flash that knocked me to the ground.

"Bryce!" I was on my knees, screaming and praying. "Bryce!"

There was nothing but the sound of falling debris and crackling wood.

"Ashley, we're over here!"

"Bryce?"

About 30 yards away I found my brother on the ground. He had fallen on top of someone, and as he leaned back, I saw the eyes of a little girl. Her face looked no older than Dylan's. While she was taller, she was so thin that she looked like a skeleton.

Bryce picked her up like she was as light as a leaf. "She can't walk, Ash." Bryce's chin quivered. "They were going to . . ."

The girl had an arm around Bryce's neck now. She looked back at the burning house and shuddered.

"It's okay," I said, more to Bryce than to her. "You're safe."

"I'm hungry," the girl said.

CHAPTER 83

☻ *Bryce* ☻

By the time the fire trucks arrived, the house had burned to the ground. An officer took the girl, who said her name was Stacy, to his squad car and called for an ambulance.

Stacy was eight, though she looked a lot younger. She said that at their last house she'd tried to get away, but her mom and dad had locked her in the closet. Some days they fed her. Some days they didn't. I couldn't imagine what she had been through.

Ashley kept saying, "It's okay. You're safe now."

Stacy said Matt had sneaked snacks to her when their parents weren't there.

"Why didn't he let you out?" I said.

"They said if he did or if he tried to get help, something bad would happen to me."

No wonder Matt was so upset when we showed up.

The ambulance came, along with a woman from a child-and-family agency. She kept shaking her head and telling Stacy she didn't have to worry anymore.

On the police radio someone said they'd caught several cars heading toward I-25. The people were being taken into custody.

"What about Matt?" Stacy said.

"He's safe," the officer said. "He'll meet you at the hospital."

CHAPTER 84

Ashley

I couldn't help thinking about what might have happened if Bryce hadn't gotten out of the house. That kept me awake after Sam and Mom picked us up.

As soon as I woke up the next morning, though, something rolling around in my brain kicked in. "The trees!" I said.

I rushed into Bryce's room and woke him.

We dressed and hurried outside, and Sam offered to drive us. I ran to the barn and grabbed a shovel.

"The police called this morning," Sam drawled. "Those two guys who were the drivers of the illegals were at that house last night. They're both behind bars."

I directed Sam to the site where we'd helped the people trapped in the truck. I took the shovel past our crumbling tree house and found the patch of ground that looked like a grave.

I dug furiously and Bryce joined in with a long stick.

We'd dug a good two feet, and my arms were getting tired. I was almost ready to give up when my shovel hit something hard.

We scraped dirt from around a box, which turned out to be a big suitcase. It had a combination on the front—six numbers. I groaned, thinking we'd have to turn the thing over to the police and would never get to see what was inside, but Bryce took my shovel, mashed it between the edges, and twisted. One side popped open.

"Money!"

More than I had ever seen in my life. One-hundred-dollar bills in stacks.

CHAPTER 85

◑ *Bryce* ◑

The police told us later how much money there was, and I couldn't believe it. There were some names and phone numbers of other drug dealers inside, which helped the police catch even more people, including the guy Ashley called White Shoes, who had set up the illegal-alien transport.

The two drivers were charged with attempted murder since some of the people in the truck almost died. I guess transporting illegal aliens was a side business for these people, like a weekend job.

I never saw Matt or his sister again, though I did read about them in the paper. The report said "two juveniles were placed in a foster home," or something like that. I was glad Matt and his sister could finally be together.

About a week later the phone rang, and Mom handed it to me.

"Timberline?" It was Matt. "I heard you and your sister helped save us. I wanted to say thanks."

"I'm sorry about . . . your parents and everything."

"Yeah. Stacy says to say hi too. She thinks you're cute."

I laughed and heard Stacy giggle. "You coming back to school?"

"Not in Red Rock," Matt said. "They moved us . . . well, I'm not supposed to say where. Guess I won't see you again. Won't be able to take you up on that plane ride you talked about."

I stood there trying to think of something profound to say. Something about God caring for us, even in the darkest moments. A verse. A sermon. But all I said was "Take it easy."

It was the end of another mystery and hopefully the beginning of a new life for Matt and his sister. I prayed that their foster family would teach them about God and that I would see them again, even if it meant in heaven.

And I hoped Ashley would never hear that Stacy thought I was cute. She'd never let me live that down.

About the Authors

Jerry B. Jenkins (jerryjenkins.com) is the writer of the Left Behind series. He owns the Jerry B. Jenkins Christian Writers Guild, an organization dedicated to mentoring aspiring authors. Former vice president for publishing for the Moody Bible Institute of Chicago, he also served many years as editor of *Moody* magazine and is now Moody's writer-at-large.

His writing has appeared in publications as varied as *Reader's Digest, Parade, Guideposts,* in-flight magazines, and dozens of other periodicals. Jenkins's biographies include books with Billy Graham, Hank Aaron, Bill Gaither, Luis Palau, Walter Payton, Orel Hershiser, and Nolan Ryan, among many others. His books appear regularly on the *New York Times, USA Today, Wall Street Journal,* and *Publishers Weekly* best-seller lists.

Jerry is also the writer of the nationally syndicated sports story comic strip *Gil Thorp,* distributed to newspapers across the United States by Tribune Media Services.

Jerry and his wife, Dianna, live in Colorado and have three grown sons and three grandchildren.

Chris Fabry is a writer and broadcaster who lives in Colorado. He has written more than 40 books, including collaboration on the Left Behind: The Kids series.

You may have heard his voice on Focus on the Family, Moody Broadcasting, or Love Worth Finding. He has also written for Adventures in Odyssey and Radio Theatre.

Chris is a graduate of the W. Page Pitt School of Journalism at Marshall University in Huntington, West Virginia. He and his wife, Andrea, have been married 23 years and have nine children, a bird, two dogs, and one cat.

RED ROCK MYSTERIES

BRYCE AND ASHLEY TIMBERLINE are normal 13-year-old twins, except for one thing—they discover action-packed mystery wherever they go. Wanting to get to the bottom of any mystery, these twins find themselves on a nonstop search for truth.

CP0140